THEY CALL ME THE MERCENARY

#3

FOURTH REICH DEATH SQUAD

Books by Jerry Ahern

The Survivalist Series
#1: Total War
#2: The Nightmare Begins
#3: The Quest
#4: The Doomsayer
#5: The Web
#6: The Savage Horde
#7: The Prophet
#8: The End is Coming
#9: Earth Fire
#10: The Awakening

The Defender Series
#1: The Battle Begins
#2: The Killing Wedge
#3: Out of Control
#4: Decision Time
#5: Entrapment

They Call Me the Mercenary Series
#1: The Killer Genesis
#2: The Slaughter Run
#3: Fourth Reich Death Squad
#4: The Opium Hunter
#5: Canadian Killing Ground

THEY CALL ME THE MERCENARY

#3

FOURTH REICH DEATH SQUAD

JERRY AHERN

SPEAKING VOLUMES, LLC

NAPLES, FLORIDA

2012

THEY CALL ME THE MERCENARY

FOURTH REICH DEATH SQUAD # 3

ISBN 978-1-61232-209-4

Dedication

For Jerry Buergel, a longtime buddy with a job that would give the "one-eyed man" second thoughts . . . All the best, pal.

Any resemblance to persons, governments, businesses or governmental entities living, dead, or operating or having operated, is purely coincidental.

Chapter One

Hank Frost thought that for once in his life he actually looked presentable – a new black patch on his left eye, his dark brown hair combed, dark blue three-piece suit clean and pressed and black loafers shiny. In fact, he thought, he was dressed quite similarly to the man standing just outside the pneumatic doors leading into the main floor of the passenger terminal, right down to the bulge under the left armpit. Frost wasn't terribly worried – a lot of people in the Chicago area carried guns, though admittedly not many did around O'Hare Field because of the relative efficiency of the metal scanners installed in the vast halls leading to the flight gates.

Frost snapped up the collar on his London Fog

raincoat and turned back toward the specially built Lincoln Continental limousine, gave a nod to the other two men on the security detail with him, and then took up a guard position a few feet away from the door through which their current charge would exit the car.

Pete Rocca got out first, taking a position flanking the door by the trunk side opposite Frost. Then Doctor Shalom Balsam stepped out. Balsam was in his middle sixties, a bit potty and possessed of an amazingly full shock of curly white hair. Gold wireframed glasses—obvious bifocals—that constantly seemed to slip down the bridge of the professor's nose gave Balsam the appearance of some old Jewish sage. Frost reflected that the latter was relatively appropriate since Balsam was old, Jewish and beyond two Ph.D.s, considered generally one of the most astute persons in the field of European geopolitics.

As Balsam stepped out onto the Pavement— Frost's good right eye ever once leaving the man he'd spotted with the gun—Frost said, "Professor—let's get inside quickly; the driver can take care of the luggage."

"Excellent, Captain Frost," was the reply, the voice seemingly brimming with Balsam's usual unflagging cheerfulness and politeness. His voice dropping then, Balsam added, "You are watching that man there wearing the blue suit, standing by the doors? Is this not so, Captain?"

Frost glanced toward the professor for a moment, started to say, "How did—" but was cut off in mid-sentence.

"You do not survive four years in a Nazi concentration camp, Captain, without developing some degree of perceptive vigilance — you can almost smell danger after a time. I'm sure a man in your profession has that ability. I'll walk quickly."

Joe Krebski, the third man in the team, was already out of the car on the other side and moving around the front of the vehicle to join them. But without waiting for the other security man, Frost started Balsam toward the airport terminal doors, his right hand momentarily touching the professor's elbow, then slipping back under his coat to the butt of the Metalifed Browning High Power hanging diagonally in the Jerry-Rig shoulder holster under his left arm. The "third safety" removable hook and pile fastener strap was in his pocket, and as his fingers closed around the checkered rubber Pachmayr grips, his right thumb loosened the thumb break so all that held the gun in the leather was the trigger guard snap.

Then two shots rang out, and Frost had his Browning out of the leather before the third. Bitterly, Frost realized he'd fallen for an old dodge. The man in the blue suit with the shoulder holstered gun had been a set-up to keep Frost's attention while other attackers had prepared to initiate the actual assault. The man in the blue suit fired a two shot burst, both rounds apparently missing. Frost fired back, the 115-grain gilding metal-jacketed, hollow-point 9mms from the Browning in his right fist spitting dead on, the twin impacts thudding against blue suit's chest and hammering him back against the concrete wall and down.

Frost started to shout, but it was too late. Rocca

had already pushed Professor Balsam through the open pneumatic doors into the outer vestibule area. Frost started for the doors himself, then ducked. A submachine gun burst from behind him ripped into the upper portion of the doorframe. As Frost went for the doors they were already closed, the electrical connections severed with a shower of sparks. Frost wheeled, still in a crouch, and snapped off two shots toward the subgunner—a man in a leather jacket standing behind the open trunklid of a taxicab by the curb.

Looking back toward the shatterproof glass doors, Frost could see Balsam trapped between the inner and outer doors, all the doors apparently on the same interrupted circuit. And less than thirty feet behind Belsam there were two college student types coming at a dead run, guns in hand.

"Hank!" Frost turned. It was Pete Rocca, both hands clutched to his blood-stained stomach, his body lurching back against the sealed shut glass doors, then curling up and rolling forward, a .45 Government Model falling from his limp, dead fingers.

"Shit!" Frost muttered. The firing was more intense now, the obvious aim to pin down Frost and the one remaining security man—Krebski—until the terrorists inside the airport could get to Balsam through the other set of doors and kill him.

Frost started toward the railing separating him from the next bank of pneumatic doors. There was a long noisy burst of automatic weapons fire, almost inaudible though over the screaming and frightened shouts of the passengers scrambling out of the way of the gunfire. Frost pulled his head down.

Glancing inside, he could see the two young terrorists less than five feet beyond the interior doors. In a moment they'd be through them and over the divider, then killing Balsam.

Almost angrily, Frost looked around. A luggage cart, abandoned by some prudent redcap when the shooting started, was less than six feet away from him. Rolling the dead Rocca aside, Frost got to his feet and jumped toward it, a hail of bullets tearing into the concrete sidewalk near his feet, then hammering into the cart as he pressed himself behind it.

Bracing it with his foot for leverage, he spun the cart on two wheels, then ran with it before him toward the double doors, smashing the heavy gauge steel cart with its full luggage load into the glass and through. In front of him, he could see Balsam fall to the floor, but Frost couldn't tell if the old professor was hurt or just ducking out of the way.

As Frost let go of the cart it kept on moving, bouncing toward the interior glass doors, then stopping. Now the two young terrorists were less than two yards away from him. Frost opened up with his Browning.

He emptied four shots into the farthest of the two men—the one with the small, pistol-sized submachine gun (an H-K Frost half-thought) then turned the gun in his cwn hand on the nearer man, the one with the pistol. Frost's Browning barked twice, only one of the shots connecting with the target and not looking to be a solid hit. The Browning's slide was locked back, the pistol empty as Frost dove now toward the young terrorist's gunhand.

11

There was a shot and Frost felt a searing pain in his left thigh but didn't go down. As his left knee started to buckle, he slapped his right hand toward the side of the terrorist's head and grabbed at the left ear, half ripping it away from the man's head as he brought him down. Using his right fist like a hammer, Frost raked it back across the terrorist's face. His hand already bloody from the near severed ear, Frost's own blood mixed with that of the terrorist as his knuckles smashed into the man's teeth, splitting open the terrorist's lips against them. Though his left leg was paining him, Frost got himself to his feet. As the young terrorist on the floor started to move, Frost lashed out savagely with his right foot, catching the terrorist's nose at its base and driving the bone up and into the brain, killing the young man instantly.

Frost stood there a moment, breathing hard, sirens wailing in the distance. As the one-eyed man turned around, he could see Krebski standing in the smashed glass littering the doorway, and he could see Balsam starting to get to his feet, apparently unhurt.

Frost walked the few steps to where his gun had fallen and picked it up. He dumped out the spent magazine and pocketed it. Then, pulling a fresh magazine from the off-gun side pouch of his Jerry-Rig shoulder holster, he rammed the fresh load up the butt of the silver-looking Browning pistol and worked the slide release, chambering a round. Frost didn't bother lowering the pistol's hammer, just upped the safety, and walked over to stand beside Balsam. Some of the terrorists who'd run away or had been driven off were still in the airport, and until the police arrived, Frost had no intention of leaving Balsam's side.

Without looking, Frost rasped to the older man, "You weren't imagining things when you called Diablo Protective Services. You have any idea who they were?"

He heard the old man beside him sigh heavily, then say, "I have a very good idea, Captain Frost. They were members of a death squad working for what I fear may be the viable threat of a Fourth Reich. The killers were Nazis, Captain Frost—Nazis, Gott in Himmel."

Chapter Two

"What are you going to do?" Frost said, glaring at the airport doctor and the brightly shining stainless steel scissors in his hand.

"I'm going to cut your trouser leg to get at that leg wound, Mr. . . ?"

"Frost — and this is my best suit. I can get a bullet hole repaired maybe, but not a whole trouser leg — I'll take my pants off." Frost swung his legs over the side of the table and dropped to the floor, wincing a little as his left leg took part of the pressure of his weight. A nurse stepped forward and tried helping him as he undid his belt and opened his fly, then dropped the pants to the floor. Swinging back up onto the table he felt he looked ridiculous — as ridiculous as anyone would look wearing

14

a three-piece suit without pants. The nurse helped him off with his coat and made to help him with the shoulder rig but he waved her away.

"Now, I'm going to give you a shot here to desensitize the skin before I give you a shot to kill the pain," the doctor said, talking to Frost's wounded thigh more than to his face.

"No—just the one to desensitize the skin—I've got a plane to catch for Paris and there could be another attempt on Dr. Balsam's life. I can't be groggy."

The doctor glanced up at Frost's face and their eyes met. "You know, this is going to hurt, Mr. I can't afford you jumping around when I'm probing."

"Just do it as fast as you can and I'll be cool— I gotta right to refuse treatment." The doctor glared at Frost, touched a needle to the skin of his left leg, and waited a moment, Frost guessed, for the numbing to take effect. As the doctor began to probe the wound, Frost simply stared up at the acoustical tile ceiling, finding something to concentrate on the only way he could resist the pain as the doctor examined his leg. The bullet had exited, Frost knew, but the doctor was searching for fragments. The doctor's voice interrupted his inspection of the ceiling. "Have you always been a bodyguard?"

"It's called executive protection," Frost said, gritting his teeth.

"Were you a cop before?"

"No—I'm,—" Frost winced—"I'm a professional soldier—you'd call it a mercenary. I work for—" the probe made Frost jump with the suddenly height-

15

ened pain—"Diablo Protective Services between assignments. You almost through?"

"Yeah—not much longer now. Tell me about it—how you get into being a mercenary? I was a doctor in the Army for a couple years—couldn't stand it."

"Well," Frost groaned, "after Viet Nam I tried going into high school teaching—English. That's what I'd trained for in school. Almost killed a student who was trying to rape a teacher—got me canned. Tried my hand," Frost winced, "hand at, ah—at being a truck driver, private detective. Started drinking too heavily, got disgusted with the civilian life and myself, and got a job over in Rhodesia at my old rank."

"What . . . Captain, isn't it? Were you Special Forces?"

"Yeah, did all that good shit." Frost glanced at the nurse, saying, "Sorry. Yeah, but after the war, with the eye gone and all, I was just another disabled vet—a lot of them out there."

"You lost the eye in Nam?" the doctor asked.

Smiling, despite the pain, Frost said, "Well, not much of a story really. You want to hear about it?"

"Sure, if you don't mind telling me—I'm almost through here."

"Thank God for small favors—well the eye . . . Anyway, like I said, not much of a story really. Happened in Viet Nam, oddest thing too," Frost groaned, shifting his weight against the operating table surface.

"No fragments and clean—just let me get some

medication on this and bandage it up ... now this should sting a little but it won't last – "

"Agh!" Frost shouted, then looking at the doctor, said, "A little, huh?"

"Anyway, tell me about the eye, huh?"

"Yeah," Frost groaned. "Well, I'd knocked out this VC machine gun nest single-handedly and General Nicholas Uissance was in the area on an inspection tour – to make a long story short he decided to give me a medal. Nothing big, you know. Well, the ceremony was to be the last ceremony the General would perform. Kind of old, ready for retirement and horribly nearsighted. So, I'm standing there at attention and the general comes up right in front of me – I could tell it was General Nicholas Uissance. Always wore his nameplate. His son, Manfred, was in the service too, so the General's nameplate read, "N. Uissance." So, anyway, his adjutant handed him the medal and the general took it, fumbled with the pin. Guess he must have thought I was a lot taller. I remember him squinting and then sticking the medal out and pinning it on me. Missed my uniform blouse completely. Naturally, despite the pain, I remained at attention until the formation was dismissed. By that time, there was just too much retinal damage."

The doctor looked at Frost, looking up from the completed bandage. "I hope your leg hurts!"

Later, more conscious of the hole in his trouser leg than the gunshot wound, Frost limped his way from the medical office down the interior hall to the Airport Security Office. Dr. Balsam, Krebski and two of the airport security men were there,

17

along with another man Frost did not recognize. Krebski said, "Hank, this is Art Lane, Diablo sent him over to substitute for Pete Rocca. How you doin'?"

"Okay," Frost grunted, easing himself into a seat opposite one of the large metal desks. Then, looking up at Krebski as he lit a Camel in the blue yellow flame of his battered Zippo, he said, "You make new arrangements, Joe?"

"Yeah, the airline was happy to help. We're leaving in about an hour. Got some Chicago cops outside that want to talk with you first—don't look like any big hassle."

"Right," Frost groaned, getting to his feet and limping toward the doorway. He was cold, sweating profusely. As he reached the door, Frost was beginning to doubt the wisdom of skipping the shot the medic had offered. Balsam's voice brought him to attention.

"You do not look well, Captain Frost—perhaps you should go to the hospital?"

Forcing a smile, Frost looked at the older man, saying, "I'll be fine once I get to sit down—tell you one thing. I'm really looking forward to a drink though once we get on board. Don't worry."

At that, Frost went through the doorway. Walking down the empty hallway, he mentally prepared for the questions the Chicago police would have for him. As he looked through the doorway into a cafeteria-like lounge beyond the hallway, the first question a uniform watch commander asked didn't disappoint him. "Captain Frost, I'd like to see your identification with Diablo Security. Do you have a blue card for your gun?"

18

"Bullshit," Frost said and sat down at one of the long metal tables, the watch commander still standing there but now staring at air.

"What did you say?" the florid faced man in his late fifties asked.

"I said, 'bullshit.' You know who I am, who I work for—you're just looking for an excuse to lift my gun. Diablo is licensed in Indiana, I'm here on official business with a State of Indiana Concealed Weapons Permit. Diablo is licensed in Illinois, too— and I'm on official business for my company."

"That doesn't necessarily allow you to carry a gun in Illinois, Frost."

"Well, that doesn't necessarily allow you to lift my gun either—we could stay in court for the next five years over that. If I hadn't had a gun, Dr. Shalom Balsam, a very prominent. Chicago citizen, would have been dead and likely several innocent by-standers, too. You lift my rod, I go to the papers and make you look like an ass."

At that Frost slowly reached under his coat, broke the Browning High Power from the leather and offered the gun, butt first, toward the watch commander.

The man stared, his face getting almost beet red. Then he picked up his hat with the gold checker-board pattern on the front that made him look, to Frost's thinking, like an overdressed cab driver, and stomped away into the hall.

A plainclothes officer walking past Frost gave him a slight nudge against the shoulder. Frost, hearing the unmistakable sound of a chuckle, laughed too as he stood up, then winced with the pain in his leg. It was becoming less intense but no more pleasant. As he walked back toward the security room the thought crossed his mind that out of the many Chicago police officers he knew, most were good guys and friends. A few, on the other hand, were turkeys like the watch commander he'd just put down—the kinds of guys who reasoned that since it was easier to arrest or generally hassle non-criminals that was what they should do with their time. Criminals were too hard to find and played dirty right back at you.

After rejoining Krebski and Doctor Balsam and the new man—Lane—Frost made his way to a private lounge the airline had reserved for VIPs—closed now to everyone but Frost's party—and sat out the half-hour before boarding the trans-Atlantic flight in relative silence.

Once aboard the flight and airborne, Frost noticed that Balsam seemed absorbed in a small paperback book inside an elegant looking leather false cover, so he turned his face toward the aisle and closed his eye . . .

Balsam awakened him. "Captain Frost—you've been sleeping," the old man said unnecessarily.

Looking around a moment and getting his bearings, Frost winced as he moved his leg. "It pains you much, Captain?" Balsam asked, his voice sympathetic.

"Only hurts when I don't laugh," Frost answered. "What have you been reading so avidly?" he asked, changing the subject.

"Oh, this," Balsam said, gesturing with the book.

The stewardess arrived with their trays—Frost didn't remember ordering, assuming Balsam had ordered for him—and just as quickly left. "Science fiction novel—SF we say."

"Not sci-fi?"

"No, Captain Frost, that is not the *cognoscenti* term. Putting myself into another, alien world, even for a few moments with one of these, has proven immensely relaxing over the years—I use the leather book covers to protect my image." Balsam laughed and Frost laughed with him.

As they ate side-by-side, the casual conversation they held turned, almost inexorably Frost felt, to the attack at the airport in Chicago, now "light-years" behind them, it seemed. "But why you, Doctor? Why not the Israeli Prime Minister, or a prominent rabbi, perhaps?"

"The answer is very simple, Captain," Balsam said, shrugging the wire-rimmed glasses from the bridge of his nose and taking an over-large blue bandanna handkerchief from his pocket to daub at the lenses. "I have become somewhat of a symbol. If you ask any Jew what he thinks about Nazis, he'll likely tell you the same thing—they were demons, butchers . . . the list of adjectives is endless. But they seem to refer to them always in the past tense. A few men—the Nazi-hunters among them—realize that for the Nazis there is no sense using the past tense. Whatever number reich they call it, it is the same, and some of the leaders are in fact the same. There are more Nazi war criminals running loose than you or anyone else—including most Jews—would imagine."

21

"Most of the big ones have been—"

"That is not true, but a common misconception. Many of the bigger ones, as you put it, have been captured or killed. But many of the lesser known men who were of equal importance during the old regime are still alive, and these men today are more vastly powerful than you would imagine. And then, everyone just remembers the Jews they killed—what about the non-Jewish Poles and Ukranians? They killed six million Jews, but they killed at least as many non-Jews. It is too easy for someone to say that hunting Nazis is a Jewish problem."

Frost, swallowing a bite of Chicken Kiev quickly so he could interject a thought, said, "But still, why you—you're not a Nazi-hunter?"

"No—but I am someone who tries to make the world aware that there are Nazis still in existence who plan once again to put the world beneath their heel—and most importantly, that the Nazis are not merely a threat to the Jews but to all men in all nations. That, Captain Frost, is why they try to kill me—in order to silence that message. But they cannot. If I am to die, then I am to die—I am an old man. But there are others who will say what I say."

Frost, sipping at his coffee, said, "But what can a bunch of senior citizen veterans of the Third Reich really do? I mean, sure there are a lot of crazies strutting around, calling themselves Nazis these days, but there aren't enough of them—"

"Captain Frost—I believe you told me you majored in English in University, with history as well."

"Yeah," Frost said.

"Remember the words then of Santayana? Something like, those who do not learn the lessons of history shall be forced to relive them. Remember your history. There were comparatively few Nazis when Hitler became chancellor in 1933, far fewer in the early years before that. They were laughed at with the beer hall putsch, and Hitler was jailed. Just a crackpot. Look at the men in the United States and in France and elsewhere who today call themselves Nazis. Crackpots? Today, perhaps, but what will they be tomorrow?

"It is," Balsam continued, "what we see today, just the tip of the iceberg—the iceberg of international right-wing terror and an eventual bid for power. They are well-financed, both by the old guard Nazi supporters and some funds from Third Reich investments. There are other rich and powerful men today who support the neo-Nazi movement. Many of them, their fathers died fighting Hitler the first time. They have arms—as sophisticated as any of the smaller third world nations—and a much easier time getting more when they need them. You would be surprised, Captain Frost, if you saw a tenth of the reports that come across my desk. That is why I go to Paris."

"The meetings?" Frost queried. "They're to organize support against the neo-Nazi movement?"

"More than that—there is support, and it is somewhat organized already, but it needs direction, purpose. And that is why I go to Paris. There is no time to delay if a counteroffensive to neo-Nazism is to be begun and successfully sustained."

Frost nodded, agreeing with Balsam but silently

thinking Balsam—perhaps because of his years in the concentration camps, perhaps just because he was a Jew—was vastly overexaggerating. Bess, the girl he'd fallen in love with, the television journalist he had rescued from death at the hands of the Nugumbwean terrorists while on his vendetta to kill Colonel Chapmann, was also Jewish. She was still based in London. Level-headed to the point of the ridiculous, Frost mentally decided to contact her when he was in Paris. He had planned to anyway. And perhaps then she could tell him more about Balsam's fears. But to Frost now, it was hard to imagine anywhere near the strength in the neo-Nazi movement that Balsam suggested.

Still favoring rum and Coke since the time spent in Mexico recovering from the wounds he'd received when President Aguillara-Garcia was assassinated, Frost ordered one from the stewardess as she went past. Checking the black-faced Omega on his wrist against their ETA in Paris, he decided he could allow himself two drinks before disembarking. As he took the first sip of the dark liquid, he smiled. The drink was well made, which was a blessing because if Balsam were only ten percent correct in his assessment of Nazis gunning for him, Frost predicted there would be little chance for drinking or anything else once they were on French soil. He closed his eye and leaned back. It was Meyers Rum—he liked that.

Chapter Three

It was cold in Paris as they left the plane. And as often as Frost had gone there, it had never been in the spring. Never once had he spied Gene Kelly dancing beside the Seine. Never had he even visited the Eiffel Tower. Frost thought that with his luck, it would probably be closed for renovation if he ever did get there.

They were expected, of course, so getting their personal weapons through French Customs was not a problem. A chauffeur, representing Diablo Protective Services, was there to meet them with a limousine, much like the one they'd left in Chicago, only in Europe a Mercedes, rather than a Lincoln. The 9mm UZI submachine guns were in the trunk, in appropriately-innocuous-looking briefcases which held spare thirty-round magazines in the event of a major terrorist attack resulting in a fire-fight. Because of their late arrival, instead of going to the smaller, lesser-known yet equally posh hotel near the prestigious Georges Cinq, they motored directly to the preliminary meeting to hammer out the details for the next day's conference of European political, business, religious and educational leaders.

As the meeting went on, Frost, Krebski and Lane slept in shifts in the security staff room. When it was Frost's turn on, he left the room and, coffee cup in hand, walked down the brightly lit panelled hallway to within ten yards of the conference room doors. There he relieved Krebski. He took his chair and sat back, his head against the wall, a half burnt-out Camel in his fingertips.

Frost opened his eye and turned in the direction of the voice he heard.

"Who are you here with, *mon ami*?" The speaker was a dark man, looking to be on the short side from where Frost was sitting, more Italian in features than French, but the speech heavily accented.

"Dr. Shalom Balsam, the geopolitics expert. How about you?"

"Ahh—no one so important, merely a minister of education. But there have been threats against him, and so . . . " The Frenchman left the sentence dangling.

"Private security?" Frost queried, lighting a fresh Camel with the glowing butt of the old one, then stubbing the spent smoke out in a nearby ashtray.

"No—a branch of the French police establishment. We do this sort of thing. And you?"

26

"Private—Diablo Protective Services out of the States."

"American, then. I have always wanted to visit your country. See?" At that the Frenchman opened his coat and revealed a classic 1930s style shoulder holster, a vintage Colt .38 revolver carried butt-side up in it. "American—I got this during the war when I fought with my father in the resistance. I was twelve years old."

"How do you feel about this neo-Nazi deal?" Frost asked.

"What is the American expression—a hill from a mole hole, no?"

"Mountain out of a mole hill," Frost corrected, smiling. "Is that what you think?"

"*Oui*—oh there are some Nazis, but not many. Mostly crazy people, people looking for the thrill of doing something that they should not be doing. This sort of thing. And you?" The Frenchman lit a Players, oddly, apparently preferring the British cigarette to any of the more popular French brands.

"I don't know—some Nazis, apparently, tried getting Doctor Balsam back in Chicago—"

"Ahh, Chicago," the Frenchman interrupted. Then, holding his hands as though he carried an invisible Tommy gun, he made the sound, "Rat-at-at-at-at—"

"Yeah, fun town all right," Frost laughed. "Anyway, some Nazis tried getting my man in Chicago, didn't though. We got them."

"That is good." The conversation went on for more than an hour as Frost waited for Balsam to reappear. The talk centered mainly on America—

movies, girls, guns, even pizza. The Frenchman called thin crust pizza with sliced cheese and tomato sauce and something like sausage "Chicago style." Frost explained that in Chicago it was usually called New York style. The Frenchman was apparently an avid amateur gastronome. By Parisian time it was 4:00 A.M. and just as Frost was beginning to feel that his stomach would never recover from the discussion, the conference room doors swung open. Balsam walked through, the man beside him someone Frost vaguely recalled from a newsclip somewhere.

With Balsam in tow, Frost met Krebski and Lane halfway down the hallway—a flasher and buzzer alert system in the security room having warned the guards that their charges were reemerging, a good feature saving a great deal of embarrassment at times, Frost judged. The ride afterward to the hotel was uneventful to the point of boredom and by 5:00 A.M. Frost was stripping off his clothes and rolling into bed, a wake up call set for seven since they were to leave for the next conference at eight that same morning.

When Frost awoke, he showered and washed his hair, shaved, brushed and flossed his teeth, and cleaned the Browning High Power. With the degree of activity ever since reaching France, Frost was seriously considering that his greatest threat of death was from boredom. Slipping on the Jerry-Rig shoulder holster and sliding the Metalifed 9mm into the leather, he pulled on his coat and went downstairs to get a quick breakfast. After downing a small steak and two eggs, croissants and coffee and orange juice — the prices amazed him — Frost took the stairs back up to Balsam's suite on the sixth floor. Krebski had taken the tour outside Balsam's door for the brief sleep period. Lane, rubbing the sleep from his eyes, his face cut from what looked like a hasty shave, was there as well.

"Balsam ready yet?" Frost asked.

"Yeah, stuck his head out five minutes ago and said he'd be ready to go soon. The chauffeur's got the car around front already." Frost just nodded, leaning against the wall beside the doorframe, then fished in his pockets and found a nearly empty package of Camels, pulled the last cigarette from it and lit it with the Zippo. By the time the cigarette was less than a half-inch long and Frost was stubbing it out in the ashtray beside the elevator, Balsam appeared. Almost unable to keep his eye open without rubbing it, Frost yawned, walked over toward Balsam and said, "Good morning, Doctor."

As Balsam yawned in return, Frost smiled. "Glad to see you're human, too. Lane, hit that elevator button."

A scream, higher pitched than you'd usually associate with a man in agony, came from behind him. Wheeling around, Frost saw Lane, his left index finger seemingly rivetted to the elevator button, his back arched, his face twisted in pain, his body writhing in an up and down motion that took his heels off the floor half the time, his clothing and neck starting to smoke.

As Krebski started to reach for Lane, Frost shouted, "Leave him! High voltage." Already, Frost's right hand was snaking under his coat for the Brown-

29

ing High Power. Then the elevator door was opening. Stepping in front of Balsam to shield him, Frost started shooting before the three terrorists in the elevator could open fire.

The 115-grain gilding metal jacketed hollow point 9s from Frost's pistol bit hard twice into the chest of the lead gunman, a second man armed with an identical submachine gun right behind him firing nevertheless. Frost pivotted, bringing the muzzle of the Browning on line for number two. From the corner of his good eye he could see Krebski, his feet spread and torso coiled into a classic combat crouch, firing a nickel-plated Colt Government .45 that was tightly clenched in both fists. Before Frost could shoot, the second terrorist went down.

Frost and Krebski both lined up on the third man, a burst from the subgun in his hands chewing a hole into the wall beside Frost's head as Frost and Krebski fired simultaneously. The impacts from two angles at once, two hits apiece as best Frost could judge, lifted the gunman off his feet and hurtled him against the far corner of the elevator, the subgun firing through the elevator flooring as the assassin slumped down dead.

Turning, Frost put two rounds from his pistol into the lock of Balsam's hotel room door, then taking a half step back, kicked in the door with his right foot, pulling Balsam in beside him. There was a sound of smashing glass and Frost wheeled. A swarm of terrorists were coming through the suite's living room window, off what looked like a window washer's scaffolding, pistols in their hands. Frost fired point blank into the nearest man, the Browning in his right hand, using his left hand to push Balsam to cover on the floor behind a couch.

The first gunman went down, the slugs from Frost's 9mm pistol apparently drilling right through him—he fell forward, knocking Frost off balance. Then, as Frost stepped back, recovering his footing, a second terrorist dove toward him.

Hitting Frost squarely in the chest, the terrorist drove him back. Both Frost and the assassin flipped over the couch. Pulling himself to his knees, Frost grabbed the man by the throat with his left hand, then hammered his right fist square into the center of the man's face. Still kneeling, Frost wheeled, slapping his left elbow into the side of the assassin's forehead.

On his feet, his gun now lost somewhere behind the couch, Frost turned. A third terrorist was less than six feet from him, the muzzle of a silenced Mauser HSc levelled at Balsam's head. Frost, no time even for the Gerber knife inside the waistband of his trousers, dove straight for the gunman, knocking the pistol off line. As Frost's left hand found the terrorist's gunhand wrist, there was a muffled cough-like sound. Frost glanced down; there was a bullet hole in the rug less than an inch from his foot.

Raking the knuckles of his right fist across the terrorist's face and driving him back, Frost smashed upward with his right knee, catching the gunman in the groin. Frost felt the rush of air from the man's mouth as the pain caught him and he doubled over. His right hand went for the terrorist's gunhand, both fists now locked on the wrist and driving the

31

gun upward. There was another silenced shot, the bullet striking into the small crystal chandelier over their heads, glass shattering and falling in icicle-sized razor-edged shards around them.

Momentarily releasing his right hand from the terrorist's wrist, Frost smashed his right elbow back and downward into the man's neck. Then he levered the gun hand downward, driving his right knee up and into the ulnar nerve at the gunman's elbow. The pistol fell from the gunman's limp fingers.

As Frost started to pivot, his knees bucked and he fell forward, a surge of pain in his right kidney. Catching himself against the edge of an end table, Frost stayed on his feet and turned, the disarmed terrorist's left foot jabbing into his solar plexus and bending him double. As the terrorist started coming in for a knee smash, Frost, unable to straighten up, drove his left fist forward, almost losing it in the flesh of the killer's abdomen.

Falling back and catching his breath, Frost then dove toward the man, hammering his right fist forward in a haymaker, then driving his left again as hard as he could into the man's gut. The terrorist doubled forward and Frost, both hands clasped together now, smashed them down between the killer's shoulder blades, then slammed upward with his right knee. As the man's head snapped back, Frost crossed his chin with a strong left, driving him to the floor. No time to finish the terrorist, Frost wheeled. Out of the corner of his eye he'd seen Krebski fighting it out with the fourth and—Frost hoped—last terrorist. Krebski was losing. The third assassin was dead on the floor—Frost had heard

Krebski's .45 go off a moment earlier.

As Frost moved toward Krebski and the terrorist, Krebski's right leg buckled and the terrorist came up with a knee smash into Krebski's crotch. On his knees before the terrorist, Krebski's face was lined up for a perfect lethal knee smash into the nose. Diving toward them, Frost knocked the terrorist off balance and into the opposite wall. Then, gaining his own footing, lashed out with his right foot in a savate kick hard into the terrorist's chest. Wheeling, he caught the man in the ribcage with the side of his left foot.

Taking a fast step forward, Frost slashed the hard knife edge of his right hand in a karate chop against the terrorist's exposed Adam's apple. As the man lolled back against the wall, he hammered the middle knuckles of his left fist forward underhand into the man's stomach just under the rib cage, driving his right palm up into the terrorist's nose, smashing the bone with the force of the blow and ramming the splinters up into the brain. Frost turned away, his opponent dead before slumping to the floor.

Glancing toward the third terrorist, the one Frost had fought with moments earlier, he could see the man, already on his feet, coming in low, barehanded, toward Dr. Balsam. Balsam, his hands up to protect his face, was recoiling against the wall, just less than six feet from Frost.

As the terrorist ran out his charge, Frost smashed up and outward with his left foot, the toe catching the man square in the ribcage and pushing him away from Balsam. Stepping toward the assassin, Frost grabbed at the man's hair to draw his face up for a blow — and the hair came off in his hand.

"A goddamned toupe!" Frost snarled, but already the terrorist had his hands going for Frost's throat. Frost let them come, then turned sharply, left, hauling his right arm up over the terrorist's hands and breaking them away from his throat. His right elbow locked over the man's wrists, with his left Frost smashed repeated blows into the terrorist's chest. Wheeling, Frost drove his left knee upward, catching the man in the stomach rather than the groin. With his right knee, Frost smashed into the side of the man's head. Looking around him, Frost saw they were beside the windows through which the terrorists had entered the suite. Frost glanced back just in time as a vase in the assassin's hand crashed down and shattered against the side of his head. Stunned, Frost fell back a moment. As the terrorist came for him, he dodged to his left, then turning into the terrorist, hooked his left fist into the side of the terrorist's face.

Spinning the man toward him with his hands at the man's throat now, Frost once again smashed toward his groin with his knee — and this time the hit was good. As the terrorist's body buckled toward him, Frost snapped the head back and drove his right fist full into his face.

The killer sprawled backward, the glass of the half-opened window shattering around him, a stifled scream coming from his bloodied mouth as he toppled through the window. Close behind him, Frost stared out through the shattered glass, down toward the street six floors below. The killer's body hit and bounced off the window washer's scaffolding, then fell. As the terrorist impacted against the awning of a flower stall in front of the hotel, then bounced through the canvas and into the street, Frost turned away.

The room was a disaster, looking for all the world to Frost to be beyond repair. Balsam, visibly trembling, was standing though and nodded to Frost. Krebski was on his knees, clutching his stomach with both hands. Frost started into the hallway, snatching up his Browning from behind the couch as he went. There were footsteps in the corridor, but as he brought the gun to bear he saw the uniforms—police. Frost raised his hands high but didn't drop the gun—"Diablo Security!" He knew next to nothing in French, but tried saying something, "*Je suis* . . . ahh . . . *Je suis Americain*—ami! Ami! *Ami*!" He kept repeating "friend" until Balsam appeared in the doorway, waving his hands in a disgusted gesture and talking in rapid, German accented French until the police lowered their weapons.

Putting his hands down, Frost turned back toward the elevator bank. Lane was on the floor, his right hand still rivetted by the electricity to the signal button. And as Frost started toward him, the smell of Lane's burning flesh was suddenly overpowering. Shaking his head, Frost turned toward Balsam, saying, "Get 'em to turn off the damn power, Doc Balsam, for God's sake."

Then Frost rubbed his hands across his face and turned away, his stomach starting to well up into his throat.

Chapter Four

As Frost sat beside Balsam in the back seat of the Mercedes, the Uzi submachine gun now out of the suitcase and cradled in his left arm, resting on his lap, he stared out the dark-tinted window. There was considerable distortion of the image as the Parisian street scenes sped past; bullet proof—or more correctly, bullet-resistant—glass always distorts image quality. Late now for the meeting and Balsam's speech, with an escort of four French motorcycle policemen—two in front and two behind—they were moving through the streets as rapidly as traffic would permit.

Lighting a cigarette, he still did not feel like saying anything to Balsam. In the intervening hour between the attack and entering the car Frost had only told the man that keeping even remotely close to his advertised schedule was suicide. Now he was fighting to get the image of Lane out of his mind. The young security man had almost literally fried to death. And it was the sort of thing that was more unnerving than the most unimaginably hideous death by gunfire or other violence — because the cause was so innocuous. There was a trick a friend in CIA had said the Russians used sometimes, and the Nazis — the World War II vintage Frost bitterly reminded himself — had used before them. A needle or straight pin, dipped in curare or something similar was tucked just under a pillowcase. When the subject went to sleep at night, the needle would prick him in the face and he'd die. Things like that or the rigged elevator button scared Frost as they did any rational man. Because unless you wanted to strip your bed every night, check the flush tank for a bomb before pulling the chain, or avoid sitting down in overstuffed chairs because there could be a poison tipped spring loaded bayonet in the cushions, you were always vulnerable. Someone could always kill you. The list of ways was endless: from needling an orange to altitude pressure sensitive paper that would explode like a bomb in an unpressurized aircraft or painting the inside of a champagne glass with transparent skin contact poisons. Nodding to himself as he exhaled a thick cloud of gray cigarette smoke from his lungs, he half verbalized the words, "The list is endless."

"What is that you said, Captain Frost?"

Frost turned and faced Balsam. "Just thinking out loud — sorry." As Frost started to turn back toward the window, he heard Balsam start to speak again and looked back once more to face him.

"Do you take 'my' Nazis more seriously, my young friend?"

"What? The guys back in the hotel? Yeah, they were serious all right," Frost said, nodding. "But why didn't you just change your route back there—we don't have to go to that damned meeting. Why not have someone else deliver the address for you?"

"Let me ask you, Captain," Balsam said, smiling. "Would you let someone else deliver an address for you like the one I plan to make because you felt you must hide in fear?"

"I don't know," Frost said, stubbing out the old cigarette and nervously lighting a fresh one, "but probably not, I guess. But my death won't be a loss to the world, it—"

Interrupting before Frost could finish, Balsam said, "Are you that unfortunate a fellow that no one will mourn you?"

Automatically, Frost's mind flashed to Bess. He had to call her—for a lot of reasons.

Without waiting for an answer, Balsam said, "You are a man whose courage is highly visible—you fight, risk death with guns and knives. But old men too can be courageous. If you had seen what I saw in the camps—but I'm glad you didn't. I would not wish that on anyone. But there is a wide range of courage, and heroes are not always tall and dark and muscular like you, with guns and ready fists. Sometimes heroes may even become heroes against their better judgment, out of desperation. The important thing is not to give up. One of the men I

38

knew in the camps—a boy of fourteen you would call him, but a man in the truest sense—used to say that with his last breath he would spit in the eye of his killer. And he did as the man disembowelled him on the parade ground for not strangling an infant as he had been told to do—the child was crying and it bothered the SS man. He had a headache. But that boy—that man—that too was courage."

Frost could say nothing. The silence awkward between them, Frost started to bring up a different subject, but stopped. He could feel the chauffeur starting to brake the Mercedes 600, rapidly, see Krebski up beside the driver starting to raise the Uzi he had on the seat beside him. Frost, leaning forward into the front seat, his right knee on the open, rear-facing jumpseat that Lane had used on the ride to the hotel, craned his neck past Krebski's shoulder. One of the motorcycle policemen in front of them was already down, skidding across the pavement of the nearly deserted highway feeder, the wheels of his motor bike spinning, his right hand clasped to his left arm. The second of the two lead cyclists was fighting to control his bike, the machine careening at a crazy angle toward the right guard rail, the policeman jumping clear just before it hit and then just lying there in the road, his body twisted at a bizarre angle.

"Must be an oil slick up ahead," Frost shouted. "Do a bootlegger now—it can't get us in worse trouble."

The chauffeur shouted a grunted something or other over his shoulder toward Frost and stomped the brake pedal hard, wrenching the wheel all the way left.

The big midnite blue Mercedes started spinning, the chauffeur going down hard on the gas pedal to get them out of the turn but the wheels apparently not grabbing. The guard rail—a dozen feet or so behind the crippled police motorcycle—was coming up fast, the chauffeur cutting the wheel back and forth, trying to get the wheels straight so he could at least control the direction of the skid. As the rear end of the Mercedes impacted against the railing, Frost was pitched back against Balsam.

Looking up over the rear seat back through the window, Frost shouted, "Brace yourself again!" One of the rear motorcycle guards was coming toward the left side doors, his face beneath the helmet and protective goggles contorted in a look of fear, his white gauntletted hands twisting at the brake and gear controls of his bike in seeming madness. There was a hard thudding sound and, even through the heavy armored door panels, Frost could hear the man's muffled death scream.

"Get this thing going—now!" Frost almost screamed. As the chauffeur shot through the automatic transmission gear box from low to high then reverse, trying for traction, Frost silently wished they had been using a full-sized American car rather than the Mercedes. The 600's almost buslike length made it harder to maneuver and though it was big, the weight and bulk just weren't right for fast changes in direction.

Already, Frost could hear the whine of gunfire hammering against the pavement outside. The tires, he realized, were bullet resistant as well, but the right slug at the right velocity could still tear holes in them and the self-sealing feature wasn't limitless in its capacity.

"Get this boat moving!" Frost shouted again.

"What the hell you think I'm doing?" the chauffeur shouted back angrily. As the motor raced, the transmission drumming and thudding, Frost punched the window button and shouting to Balsam to "Stay down on the floor, Doc," opened fire in the direction of the gunshots, holding the Uzi in his fists to three-shot bursts. He could hear it before he felt it, the car starting to move. It was slipping, sliding, but moving forward. Shooting a glance over his right shoulder, Frost caught sight of Krebski, his window open, his body half extended out of the car, the Uzi in hands roaring toward the attackers. As Frost looked away he heard Krebski cry out, turned back and saw him slump, his legs still inside the car, his body hanging out through the window, his light gray suit riddled at the waist with bullet holes. And over the hump of the dead body and beyond, Frost at last spotted the terrorists—young looking from the brief look he got, dressed like workmen, European looking assault rifles of one type or another in their hands.

As the Mercedes picked up speed, Frost turned around and started firing behind them. The last remaining motorcycle cop went down then, his feet knocked from under him like bowling pins as three terrorists braced him—their assault rifles against his handgun.

Pulling his head back inside, Frost started to shout

41

to the chauffeur, but got cut off. "Yeah, I know—
step on it," the chauffeur snarled.

"What a mind reader," Frost shouted back over
the noise of the wind and the automobile engine, his
face cracking into a grin, the smile-frown lines in his
cheeks deepening.

As the Mercedes picked up speed, the terrorists
were vanishing in the distance behind the car. Just
as Frost started to verbalize the thought that they
were out of the woods, he heard the chauffeur
shouting, "Look out—my God!"

Twisting around, Frost looked toward the front
of the car. Like drums in his ears, he could hear
the clicking sounds as the chauffeur pumped at
the brake pedal, see the man starting to move his
right hand toward the gear shift—trying for reverse?
—but it would be too late. There was a huge semi—
American made, the kind moving companies use—
just ahead of them, the hydraulic lift gate extended
outward at about the level of the Mercedes' roof
line.

Frost dove down between the seats, his head
slamming against the drive shaft hump as they hit.
Before his eye closed, a sea of darkness washing
over him, he could see the roof tearing away as
though some giant child with a thirst for death
were ripping open a can of human sardines, the
blur of the driver's head, severed by the hydraulic
lift platform, flying over him—and Frost thought
he could feel tiny droplets of blood against his
own flesh . . .

Frost opened his eye, his head pounding with

42

even the smallest movement as he tried getting up. He could hear sirens in the distance—police, he thought absently. Suddenly, his mind became aware of what happened—Balsam! He moved his head too fast and almost passed out. Fighting the dizziness, he opened his eye again. But Balsam was gone. Frost raised his hand to his face—it was covered with splatters of blood. Looking down, he noticed that so were his clothes.

Slowly, he turned his head toward the front of the car. That it was the front seat of an automobile was barely recognizable. Looking over it he saw the grisly stump of neck, the ragged flesh still wet with glistening bright red blood. The head was gone—he remembered then the decapitation, the chauffeur's severed head flying over him at impact.

He looked around, absently trying to determine how best to climb from the twisted wreckage.

Mechanically, he reached into his pocket for a cigarette and stuck the butt into his mouth, but as he reached for the lighter he started to think clearly—gas fumes could go up any minute, he realized. Then he felt the thing in his pocket.

Slowly, he withdrew his hand from the side of his jacket. He knew instinctively what the thing was before he saw it, but seeing it made him admit it to himself: a man's little finger, a trickle of blood still draining from it. Attached to the flesh with a safety pin was a tiny plastic bag. Inside it was a note.

Smoothing the plastic against his thigh, Frost could make out the words there—a crude scrawl, the message in English. "Every forty-eight hours until ten million dollars in diamonds is paid, we will send back a piece of Professor Balsam. You will be contacted on how to buy back your Jew."

There was no signature, no name, but something just as distinctive and recognizable, Frost thought — a ragged, uneven series of lines drawn in what looked like Balsam's blood.

The lines formed a Swastika.

Chapter Five

"You care for some of these potatoes with your sandwich, Monsieur Frost?"

Frost didn't remember what they called them in France, but in America they were French fries and dripping with catsup, the imagery was too reminiscent of his experience in the motorcar when he'd reached into his pocket and found the note and the once living human flesh to which it had been attached.

"No," Frost said. "I'll stick with the roast beef sandwich — thanks." He looked away from the French fries — they were starting to make him sick.

Fouchard was a pleasant enough guy, Frost was thinking, but a little too friendly.

"When do you lower the boom?" Frost asked,

his mouth full and his talking a little garbled.

"What is this 'boom' you say?" Fouchard asked.

"Well," Frost said, "I shot up some French territory, probably caused you a lot of unpleasant headlines and lost a prominent visitor to France. Now you got a kidnapping to handle and a kind of a rough deadline to get up a ransom or have that prominent visitor come back in pieces. He's a hell of a good guy, Balsam, that is."

"*Oui*—that is my understanding, *mon ami*. But just because I am upset at what has happened does not require that I behave badly, that I shout, that I say that I will not let you become even the most remotely involved with this matter any further—that I confiscate this pistol," and he nodded toward the Metalified Browning on his desk, "or the knife you carry—until you leave France. This is all true, of course, but there is no need to belabour what is obvious, *oui?*"

Frost looked at the Sûreté inspector a moment, then only said, "Great roast beef—Argentinian?"

"*Oui*, I think so as well."

"Counter any good terrorists lately? We call that small talk in America."

"No—counter-terrorism work is hardly spectacular—but we do try our best. Tell me, Hank, if I may call you that. How did you lose your eye? I assume of course that this patch over your eye is a permanent fixture . . . "

"About as permanent as you can get," Frost said, finishing the last half of his sandwich and picking up the steaming styrofoam cup filled with black coffee. He sipped at it and it burned his tongue.

The taste was on the strong side as well. "Not much of a story," Frost said, his face creasing with the smile-frown lines.

"If it would not bring back the unpleasant memory, I would be interested to hear it," Fouchard said, tugging at the belt under his slightly sagging stomach and leaning back in his swivel chair, stroking his thin moustache.

"As you wish," Frost said. "Well, I always had a fascination with archeology. I was dating this girl in college –"

"Dating? What is this?"

"We were going out together – you know."

"Ahh – *oui*. Yes – continue, please."

"Well, her father – a medical doctor, had come across this map. Seemed that the Aztecs had determined to hide their most glorious treasure from Cortez when he conquered Mexico – hid it in a remote mountain area that is so far off the beaten track that to this day only some few scattered tribes of terribly savage Indians inhabit the region. It was a ceremonial mask, it was, solid gold with blue sapphires in the eyes." Smiling still, Frost went on. "Well, to make a long story short, it was summer vacation and I went along with my girl and her dad back into the primitive hill country in search of the mask of the Aztecs. The jungle was extremely dense – had to use two machetes in each hand to hack my way through. Some of the locals we had guiding us learned of the doctor's quest for the mask and believed in an ancient curse the mask carried. Let's see – how'd it go? Hmmm. Yeah – that was it! Whosoever whatfor inasmuch regardless cometh to

47

violate the hiding place of the sacred mask of the Aztecs hidden from the white conquerer shall suffer unto himself such as is done to the mask."

"This is true?" Fouchard asked, interrupting.

"Sure thing," Frost said. "Well, our guides ran off with all the supplies—including the medical supplies—all except for the doctor's bag. We pressed on, nonetheless, the fetid smell of the tropical rain forests, the snakes, the wild animals—the constant dangers and the terrible weariness beginning to tell even on Felicity—"

"Felicity?" Fouchard repeated quizzically.

"Yes, yes, the young lady of my affections—Felicity Entwhistle—father's first name was Throcmorton."

"Throc-morton?"

"Very common name back in the States—very common. Well, as I said, even Felicity was in a bad way, her usual cheerfulness all but gone. There was no way of telling how long we'd trecked, but then one morning as the mists cleared, that hellish tropical sun already starting to cook our brains under the scant protection of our pith helmets, Doctor Throcmorton Entwhistle and I had decided that we must turn back. Felicity was down by the riverside washing her little ladies things when suddenly we heard this bloodchilling scream. I can't even begin to describe it. Entwhistle snatched up his Jeffrey .500 double rifle and his cartridge bandolier; I grabbed my borrowed 8.43 mm Krumpnik Express and we were off.

"By the time we'd reached the stream," Frost went on, his tone breathless, "Felicity was gone, but in the soft mud beside the waters Entwhistle spied his daughter's footprints—she'd insisted on wearing high heels. And beside them, he found the footprints of the dreaded Turtle Men, the fierce tribe of aborigines legend credited with guarding the Aztec mask."

"This is true? Sacre—"

"Well," Frost went on, "we tracked the dreaded Turtle Men for three days and nights. Just as we were about to give up hope, we both heard Felicity singing—'Three Blind Mice,' I think it was. She always sang nursery songs whenever she was terrified—when she was driving her daddy's Ferrari, for example. Checking the loads in our guns we ran up the trail and there was Felicity—and beside her the golden Aztec mask—part of the Turtle Men's fiendish ritual of bloodlust. Just as they were about to bring the Anaconda in contact with Felicity's lovely body—naked as a scalded dog, she was— Entwhistle fired, cutting the snake in half.

"Seizing my machete, I ran into the hordes of savages and hacked my way toward her, cutting her bonds with a single swipe of its razor sharp edge and snatching her up into my arms. I reached down for the mask to grab it as well and as I did I dropped it. One of the blue sapphire eyes—the left one— was dislodged from its centuries old niche and rolled to the ground—lost forever.

"And then," Frost said with a dramatic flourish, "is when we realized the curse was true. That's how I lost my eye. And, it scared hell out of the natives. In fear they ran off."

"But how did you lose your eye, Frost?"

49

"Just like the mask—my eye fell out and rolled away. Damnedest thing. Refuse to believe in that superstitious rot, I used to say. Just coincidence! But was it, I wonder?" Frost asked rhetorically, lighting a cigarette and tugging meaningfully at his eyepatch.

Inspector Fouchard looked at him a moment, then said, "What is the word—yes; you are crazy." Then Fouchard's face creased into a smile and he started to laugh.

His face darkening, Fouchard said, "And since you are so good at telling stories, tell me again, Captain Frost, about the terrorist raid on the limousine."

Sighing heavily, Frost said, "I've gone over it for you and over it—how many times?"

"If you were a policeman instead of a soldier working as a security man, you would realize that this retelling of the crime can often bring to light details which in the warmth of the minute—"

"Heat of the moment," Frost corrected.

"What? *Oui*, heat—heat of the moment—English, it is very difficult. Details, which in the heat-of-the moment, have been forgotten. Now, again please."

Frost sank back deeper into his chair, but as he started to speak there was a knock on the frosted glass window of Fouchard's office door.

"*Entrez*," the inspector droned. A slightly built man, wearing a dark suit, came in with a single sheet of typing paper, handed it to Fouchard and was dismissed with a wave. "We took the fingerprint of . . . the finger . . . the one from your pocket . . .

and cross checked this with your FBI—"

"No, they're not my FBI exactly."

"At any event, the fingerprint—it matches those on file with the U. S. Department of Immigration and Naturalization. There is no mistaking it—it is the severed digit of Professor Balsam! The blood types out to be his as well—the blood used to draw the . . . the Swastika . . . on the ransom note."

There was a smaller piece of paper—a memo sheet—clipped to the typed sheet Fouchard had read from. Glancing at this a moment, Fouchard looked up at Frost. Then, saying nothing, he punched the key on the vintage intercom on his desk, and said something in French Frost was totally unable to fathom. Turning back to face Frost, Fouchard said in English, "Your Monsieur Andrew Deacon, head of Diablo Protection, is outside. I just asked for him to be sent in. Unlike the FBI, Monsieur Deacon is in fact yours?"

Smiling, Frost said, "At least temporarily." As Deacon entered the office, the door held for him by the man who had served as messenger a moment earlier, Frost said, "Hey, Andy—what's happenin'?"

Deacon, tall as a basketball player, rapier thin and expensively dressed as always, glared at Frost and muttered, "What's happenin'!"

"Monsieur Deacon, I am Inspector Maurice Fouchard of the Sûreté."

"I bet you thought he was the cleaning lady," Frost said, smiling.

Fouchard turned and glared at Frost a moment, then continued, "I am sorry that we must meet under such unpleasant circumstances, Monsieur Deacon."

"Let's cut the crap, Inspector What's-his-name," Deacon said, sitting down across from the still standing Fouchard and bracing his size thirteen left foot against the edge of the desk.

Fouchard, still standing there, forced his smile visibly, reached into his upper left desk drawer a moment and then extended his right hand toward Deacon's foot, the object from the desk drawer still in Fouchard's hand but not fully visible. There was a loud clicking noise and the eight inch blade of what Frost would have labeled a Mexican Push-button—the kind where the blade comes straight out of the handle with a forward motion rather than swinging out of the side—appeared. Fouchard said, "If I am to cut the crap, as you say, Monsieur Deacon, where would you wish me to start?"

Frost laughed out loud, then touching his right index finger to his lips etched five hashmarks into the air, saying, "Five points, Inspector Fouchard—Deacon has the ball."

"Shut up!" Deacon rasped, glaring over his shoulder at Frost. Then turning back toward Fouchard, he spread his palms outward and smiled, saying, "I'm sorry if I came on kind of strong, Inspector. I was in West Berlin when I heard about the first attack at the hotel, changed my reservations to get here and by the time I was off the plane the news of the second attack and the loss of Doctor Balsam was all over the place—doesn't make for a good corporate image."

"Didn't do a heck of a lot for Balsam's image, either," Frost added, "especially his left hand."

"I am glad that you are here, really, Monsieur

Deacon. Your Captain Frost has been most helpful. As I mentioned to him a moment earlier, before you arrived, I am keeping his gun and his knife until he is boarded on a plane out of the country. I have neither the authority nor the time to force him to leave the country earlier than he might wish, of course. Captain Frost has committed no crime. But as the kidnapping of Doctor Balsam is directly under the jurisdiction of the Counter-terrorist Bureau of which I am head, I do have total authority in the running of the investigation. If you or Monsieur Frost should decide to become involved in attempting to find the good professor, I will have you arrested and subsequently deported, your visa revoked."

"I'd still have my Master Card," Frost said, laughing, then added, "I couldn't resist it, sorry."

"We want to help, Inspector," Deacon said, his voice almost pleading.

"Monsieur Deacon, though I am sure Captain Frost did his best to safeguard Professor Balsam from these Nazis or whatever they are, believe me —Diablo Protective Services has already done more than enough. Before Captain Frost arrived, I did not have a gang of heavily armed kidnappers cutting pieces off a prominent U. S. citizen, there were no gunbattles on the highways, nor slaughters in hotel rooms. No, let me assure you that Diablo has indeed done enough. I will, of course, as a courtesy, keep your company informed as to any major developments. We are agreed?"

Fouchard looked at Deacon, then to Frost and Frost pointed his right index finger back at Deacon.

There was silence for a moment, then Deacon said, "What choice is there?"

Frost and Deacon walked for a while afterwards, stopping after about fifteen minutes at a sidewalk cafe and ordering coffee. Deacon lit one of his large cigars and broke the casual silence they'd maintained. "You want to stay, right?"

"Yeah," Frost said, lighting a cigarette, sipping at his coffee and turning his head to visually follow a very pretty woman a moment.

"I can't authorize you to go against Fouchard's order—you get in trouble, you're on your own. But I'll pick up expenses for a reasonable time— try and stay out of that smart ass cop's way, huh?"

"I always like that about you Andy—you're so pleasant."

"You got any idea where you'll start," Deacon asked, ignoring Frost's jibe.

"Probably try getting together with Balsam's colleagues—the guys raising the ransom—and see where it leads me. I don't know yet. I gotta get some sleep though."

"Here," Deacon said, handing over a small dark colored wallet. "I set you up with five thousand dollars in traveller's checks. You got an American Express Card?"

Smiling, Frost started to say, "I never leave home—"

"Oh, go to hell. Look, I'm catching a cab to the airport, then heading to New York—you can reach me at the branch office there. See ya'." With that, Deacon stood up, tossed a couple of bills on the table and walked off.

Frost sat there for another twenty minutes, watching the girls, watching the street scene and trying to relax. It wasn't doing him any good. He got up and downed the last of his fourth cup of coffee and hailed a cab for his hotel.

When he entered the lobby, there were still some police there, talking with the manager, the manager glaring at Frost as he crossed the lobby to the elevator bank. Then thinking better of it—he still couldn't forget how Lane had died earlier that day—Frost walked over to the stairs and started up. As he opened his hotel room door, he spotted two small envelopes just inside on the floor. The one was from the hotel—Frost could almost imagine what it was, the other a cable. He opened the one from the hotel first.

He was surprised. Rather than an eviction note, it was a message from the operator saying that he was to meet a Mademoiselle Sheila Balsam in the hotel lobby at—he checked the black faced Omega Seamaster on his wrist. He had fifteen minutes. Quickly, then, Frost ripped open the cable envelope:

Frost:
Happy you're still alive. Come see me soon. Also, got info on your problem with Nazis. Working on allied story here or would come to you.

Love, etc.,
Bess

Frost smiled, folded the cable closed and—feeling rather foolish—put it in his wallet. Yes, he thought, got to see Bess. Also, as he stripped his clothes and headed for the shower, he wondered what information she might have for him. As he got the water right — the pressure a little erratic — and started to wash the blood from his hair and body, he realized coldly that information was exactly what he needed now. In less than thirty-six hours, unless the ransom were raised before then, another piece of Balsam would be sent as a grisly reminder that his kidnappers meant business.

And that bothered Frost — if the Nazis were so well funded, why a ransom demand? Ten million dollars in diamonds would be useful to anyone, he reasoned, but according to what Balsam had indicated about the scope of the Nazi movement, it would be a mere drop in the bucket for them. And why kidnap the man at all? Why not just kill him outright? Frost entertained no naive notions that the Nazis would release Balsam after the ransom was paid, but still . . . He turned the water straight cold and rinsed under it a moment, then stepped out of the shower, towelled and dressed.

Automatically, he started to reach for his shoulder rig, but then put it down. Fouchard still had the Browning and the Gerber knife as well. Reaching into his flight bag, Frost found his safety razor. He only used it when he was in the field, preferring his Norelco electric under normal circumstances. Extracting one of the double-edged blades and a small roll of single-faced black electrical tape he carried for emergencies, he taped over the one edge several times, effectively blunting it.

In the kit with the razor he had a small package of

toothpicks. He took several of these and placed them along with the razor blade in the vacant business card slot in his wallet, then dropped the wallet in his pocket. Tossing a black silk crocheted tie under his turned up shirt collar, Frost snatched up his jacket and left the room, again taking the stairs to the lobby as he knotted the tie about his neck, then straightened the shirt collar.

As he reached the lobby, he started scanning the people sitting there. There was only one that could have been Sheila Balsam – raven-haired, tanned, in her early to middle twenties, wearing a simple but expensive looking emerald green dress. Buttoning his coat to look more presentable and automatically straightening his tie, he left the stairwell and started across the lobby toward her.

Before Frost could say anything, the girl said, "The eyepatch – you're Captain Henry Frost . . . I'm Sheila Balsam. What are you doing to find my father?"

"Could we at least shake hands first?" Frost asked, trying to smile.

The girl ignored him, then went on with her tirade. "I thought you dummies were providing security for my father. Hell of a good job you did."

"You want to talk," Frost said, "fine – I'll talk. You want to shout, find somebody else." Frost started to walk away.

"Wait a minute," the girl said, her voice a little softer. "I'm sorry – but I've got to find my father."

"Then let's go someplace for a drink and talk about it," Frost said, reaching his hand to her elbow. She stood up and walked beside him.

"Someplace for a drink" was a bar Frost had

spotted two blocks away. With an American name, it sounded all right to him and when they entered the place, Frost thought almost for a moment that indeed he was somehow back in the States. The place was dark, the walls panelled, a long decorative bar dominating the wall to their right as he waved away the waiter who evidently wanted to find them a table. Frost found them two stools at the bar instead.

The barman was with them almost instantly. "What are you having?" Frost asked the girl.

"Gin and tonic," she told him.

"Gin and tonic for the lady then and I'll have a—let's see. Yeah, gimme a screwdriver. I can use some Vitamin C."

The bartender left and Frost turned to the girl. "Talk."

"I'll repeat what I asked before—what are you doing?"

"Right now," Frost said as the bartender brought their drinks, "I'm sharing a healthful beverage with a beautiful young lady. Later, I don't know. What you got in mind?"

"You—!" The Balsam girl started to get up and Frost put out a hand and touched her right arm to hold her.

"Wait—no sense of humor. Relax, will ya'?"

"How can you make smart remarks when my father is in the hands of the Nazis and being subjected to God knows what?"

Sighing heavily as he lit a cigarette, offering one to the girl who just shook her head no, Frost said, "Being a nervous wreck won't help anyone. I plan

58

to work as best as I can with the people raising the ransom and go from there—Sherlock Holmes I'm not, kid."

"Is that all?" Her voice kept changing in volume and pitch, her words clipped and fast—hysteria, Frost wondered?

"Unless you have a better suggestion—that Inspector Fouchard. If you haven't talked to him go and see him. Seems like a competent man and seems sincerely interested in getting your father back as quickly and safely as possible. Doesn't want my help, though." Taking a sip of his drink, Frost added, "Maybe you can change his mind? Hmm?"

She was silent for a moment, downing the gin and tonic too fast, then saying, "Order another one for me."

"Sure," Frost said, then signalled the barman and pointed to their glasses and held up two fingers.

"What do you think my father's chances are?" she asked, her voice suddenly low and frightened sounding.

"Honest, or do you want me to make you feel good?"

"Honest," she stammered.

"If we can find him, wonderful—probably a good chance of getting him back in one piece," Frost said, almost swallowing the last word when he realized what he'd said. "But," he sighed, "if we can't find them, I'm almost positive they'll kill him. Wouldn't make any sense for them to do anything else." Shrugging, Frost finished his old drink before the bartender snatched it, and then he took a sip of the fresh one.

"Can you help — I can pay," she said, her voice low.

"I'll try my best, Miss Balsam. And you don't have to pay anything. My expenses are covered. Get me in with the people raising the ransom — the people from the conference. Maybe see if you can ease things a little with the Sûreté. We'll go from there."

"All right," she said.

"Fine. I'll meet you for dinner tonight and we can make some definite plans. I'm gonna try and rack up some Z's."

"What?" she asked.

"You been away from America for a while or what?"

"I just flew in from Israel — I'm working with a joint Israeli-U. S. archaeological team down there on a dig just outside Jerusalem."

"Oh," Frost said, nodding. "Where are you staying?"

Frost arranged to meet the girl at her hotel at seven that evening, have dinner and afterward hopefully meet with the members of her father's committee. Putting her in a cab outside the bar, then turning toward his hotel, he wished that he could get some sleep, but there was something more important to do first.

Chapter Six

Frost realized that he knew next to nothing about Paris, but underworld was underworld, he optimistically hoped, and the underworld would be the only source for a gun—especially to a foreigner. CIA guys did it all the time, he understood. And crooks everywhere in the world got their guns illegally—only the honest people had to fill out forms and pay sales tax—so Frost confidently got a taxi to drop him not far from the Seine in a neighborhood that looked sufficiently corruption-ridden and hoped for the best.

The streets were narrower there, Frost observed. The sidewalks had more cracks and the signs proclaiming the business establishments were smaller and gaudier. It took him three bars in two hours to get a name and at the fourth bar he found the man.

Leaning against the rail, Frost said, "A guy named Pierre told me you could maybe help me."

"*Je ne comprende pas Anglais,*" the man said, then turned away.

Frost studied him a moment, looked at the overly flashy clothes, the poor excuse for a shave, the almost animal like wariness in the blue eyes, then said, "*Comprende* money, pal?"

The man turned around. "American?"

"*Oui,*" Frost said, proud of himself for executing so competently one of his few French expressions.

"We will talk—but not here."

"Oh, hell no—I didn't think we'd talk here," Frost said. "You go to the movies too, huh?" When the man looked at Frost uncomprehendingly, Frost said, "You know—the good guy meets an underworld crony in a bar and the guy always says, 'We will talk—but not here.'"

"Who are you?" The man was trying to make his voice sound menacing, Frost thought.

"I'm a senior vice president with a major oil company, just here on a junket and looking for exotic souvenirs. What's it matter—I need a rod."

"What is this rod thing?"

"I want to hang curtains," Frost said, smiling, "A gun, friend."

"Shh," the man whispered. Then, "All right, come with me."

As the man started away from the bar and Frost made to follow him, the man stopped, his eyes

62

rivetted on another man standing up from a far corner table. That man's mouth dropped open wide, a single word coming from it, but more like an involuntary reflex, Frost thought, than something consciously pronounced. "Gerard!"

Frost looked back and stared at the man at the far table – evidently Gerard. And Gerard was staring back. Raising his fists into the air, he screamed, "Berton!"

Suddenly, the man from the far corner – Gerard – was running toward the bar, a dark glass wine bottle in his right hand now, red wine running down his arm from the mouth of the inverted container. A huge man, he was shouting now at the top of his lungs and Frost thought he caught the word, "*Morte.*"

"Morte d' Arthur," Frost said to himself. Turning to the man beside him – Berton – Frost said, "He wants to kill you?"

Suddenly, Gerard was leaping toward Frost and Berton and Frost sidestepped away. The bottle in Gerard's hand came crashing down, missing Berton's head and smashing across his right shoulder instead. Suddenly, too, Berton seemed to come out of the paralyzing stupor of fear that had rivetted him beside the bar and reacted, a knife flashing into his hand.

As Frost edged away, he heard a shout from behind him. Turning, he saw a man twice his own size, a beer glass in his hand and beer all over the front of his work shirt. Smiling, Frost said, *"Excusez moi,"* but the big man with the beer stained shirt was already hauling back his right and Frost couldn't get out of the way.

Doing the only thing he could, Frost straight-armed the man in the solar plexus. As Frost started to edge away, he felt a hand on his shoulder.

Instinctively, Frost ducked. Out of the corner of his eye, he saw a fist passing over his head, connecting with a smallish man standing where the guy with the beer stains had been before Frost had decked him. Suddenly, there was noise everywhere. As Frost started up out of his crouch, there was another total stranger coming at him, a chair in his hands. Reaching out, Frost grabbed the man next to him — someone else he'd never seen before — and pushed the man between him and the chair.

Fists were flying everywhere, furniture crashing down, bodies smashing to the floor then getting up again to fight some more. From behind the bar, Frost could hear the bartender — Frost didn't need French to know what the man was saying, the tone saying it all.

As Frost ducked, avoiding a haymaker, he caught sight of the man who was going to sell him the gun — Berton. The knife the man had had in hand was gone and the big wild man called Gerard was holding Berton in a bear hug, trying, Frost figured, to break Berton's back.

Frost, seeing his gun going out the proverbial window, pushed his way toward the pair. Berton's eyes were starting to bulge, his face turning purple as the bear of a man crushing him squeezed the air from his lungs. Gerard's locked fists were tightening further at the small of his back. Frost snatched a miraculously unbroken bottle from the bar and smashed it down across the back of

64

Gerard's head. "My God!" Frost said. If Gerard had even registered feeling the bottle, Frost couldn't tell. And the big man's grip wasn't loosening on Berton.

Bunching both his fists together, Frost hauled them back like a baseball bat, then hammered them forward into Gerard's right kidney. There was a loud gutteral scream and Berton fell from Gerard's grasp as he sank toward the bar. As the big man turned, his fists starting to fly, Frost clamped his fists together again and swung. This time he caught Gerard on the left side of the jaw and knocked him back with such force that the big Frenchman fell back across the bar and rolled over and down behind it.

Berton still seemed stunned, and Frost just grabbed the man by his arms and started propelling him toward the glass fronted doors. Within arm's reach of the double doors, Frost stopped in his tracks — police whistles and the sound of sirens came to his ears. Wheeling, then dragging the listless Berton with him, Frost hacked his way through the flailing wall of haymakers and savate kicks and back across the barroom floor. He spotted a rear entrance, but turned instead toward the staircase leading to the mezanine-like balcony. A few treads up the stairs, Frost grunted, "Hell!" and bent his left shoulder down into Berton's midsection and hoisted the man up and onto his shoulder, then continued up the stairs.

At the head of the stairs, Frost stopped — there was a man about his own size, dressed in a gray pin-striped suit and lavender-colored shirt, blocking his way, a brightly chrome plated automatic half-swallowed in his right hand. As the man raised the gun toward him, Frost leaned forward, dropping the groggy Berton from his shoulder and into the man with the gun. As the man fell back under Berton's weight, Frost reached out with his left and pushed the gunhand off line and hooked his right fist across the man's jaw.

Catching up the pistol in his left hand then, Frost turned and made a half-salute toward Berton, muttering, "Looks like I don't need you anymore, pal." Pushing through one of the doorways fronting the small balcony, Frost raced across the empty sleeping room to the window. It was jammed and painted shut. Frost smashed his right elbow through the glass, shattering it, then knocked away the remaining jagged shards. Below was the alley, no fire escape, but no Paris police either, Frost decided, scanning the pavement below.

Climbing through the window onto a small ledge outside, Frost edged his way down onto his knees, then let himself down on his hands, swinging there a moment over the alley, then letting go and pushing himself off and away from the wall, coming down in a crouch and going into a roll.

Looking up as he got to his feet, Frost still saw no one; then, the gun in his pocket, turned and raced toward the end of the alley and into the street.

An hour later, back at his hotel, Frost sat with a cup of room service coffee and a cigarette, examing the firearm. Like most illegally obtained guns, which this obviously had been—the man Frost had taken it from looked like a pimp—the gun was flashy-looking but short on quality. A .32 ACP automatic, it was a German brand and frought with potentially greater danger for the person shooting it than the person being fired upon.

As Frost reloaded the gun, checked its poor plastic to metal fit, noted the sloppiness of the slide, he reflected that cheap in price didn't have to mean cheap in quality. Frost had used a Raven .25 several times as a hideout gun on security details. One of the least expensive firearms made, it worked more reliably and was more accurate than many similar guns costing two or three times as much. But the tiny automatic Frost now held he was not impressed with, seriously considering whether it really was better than nothing.

At a bookstore on his way back to the hotel, Frost had secured a hardbound English copy of the complete works of Shakespeare. Having read the complete works of Shakespeare, he felt little guilt turning halfway through *The Comedy Of Errors* and commencing to hollow out the rest of the book with a razor blade—just large enough to accommodate the .32.

For the third time that day, Frost reckoned, he again needed a shower. He grabbed one quickly, then changed. The Omega on his wrist read close to 7:00 P. M. as he locked the hotel door behind him, catching up his volume of Shakespeare as he went. As he took the stairway down to the lobby, again avoiding the elevator, he found himself whistling, eliciting an angry look from the hotel manager as he reached the lobby. Waving to the man, Frost walked across the lobby and outside, finding a taxi, then settling back for the ride to Sheila Balsam's hotel.

She was waiting for Frost in the lobby, wearing what he decided would be most aptly described as a cocktail dress—black, low-necked and full-skirted—with black patent leather high heeled shoes and small matching bag, and a very feminine looking crocheted shawl draped about her shoulders.

As Frost came closer to her he noticed very little jewelry—small earrings and a string of pearls and an elegant gold wristwatch. "You look lovely," he told her, honestly. He looked into her eyes for a moment—they were green. He noticed the graceful curve of her throat—her almost black hair was pinned up, and thin wisps of it that had broken free at the nape of her neck.

"You're staring at me, Captain Frost."

"You're right, Miss Balsam," Frost said, smiling. "Do you know Paris?" he asked changing the subject.

"Yes—do you?"

"Not well—is there somewhere you'd like to go?" There was: a small restaurant that was "intimate," with "exquisite cuisine." The taxi ride there was brief, and there was—surprisingly Frost thought—no wait for a table at the restaurant once they arrived. Dark, candle-lit, with flesh and blood violinists playing as they moved about the tables, it was a movie stereotype, Frost thought, and pleasant.

The menu was in French, and Frost was relatively mystified. The Balsam girl spoke French —evidenced during the taxi ride—so he asked her

68

to translate. "You don't speak any French?" she asked, her voice reflecting a tone of incredulity.

"I can say, *'Je ne comprende pas Francais'*," Frost said, smiling.

"That means you don't understand French," Sheila Balsam said.

"You got it – so tell me what the menu says." Frost settled on something that even translated seemed terribly different from the beef stew in wine sauce and buttered asparagus spears put before him, but he decided it tasted good after the first bite. He'd read novels, he recalled, where the hero always ordered Tattinger's pink champagne, so he told the girl to order that and when it arrived he decided it tasted good enough – although he usually didn't care for champagne.

Over a dessert ot tepid cherries smothering rather mushy – he thought – vanilla ice cream, Frost remarked, "Must be homemade ice cream – pretty good."

Smiling, Sheila Balsam said, "You amaze me – just wow a girl over with your continental manners, don't you?"

"Well," Frost said, his face creasing into a smile, "I just normally lead the rough, tough, rugged outdoor life of a professional soldier – all this fancy sissy food is new to me."

"Let me guess," she said. "Cheeseburgers and whiskey, right?"

"No – you misjudge me. I prefer pizzas and PBR in twelve ounce cans." Then, his smile fading, Frost said, "What do you want? I don't earn as much in a day as this meal is going to cost. And I don't have a heck of a lot of time for the finer things."

"But you seem to glory in it, don't you? What would you do if you were rich?"

"Me? I don't know—probably buy a few extra spare magazines for my pistol, maybe swap my Omega here for a Rolex," he said, gesturing to the watch on his wrist. "Buy another suit—this one's got a bullet hole in it. Stuff like that."

"What are you doing with that *Complete Works of Shakespeare* you've been carrying around all night?"

"Don't you remember the song?" Frost asked. "Brush up on your Shakespeare and the women you will wow'?"

"What?"

"Trying to wow you, like the Cole Porter song says. Want to impress you with my culture. Also wanted a place to carry the gun I've got illegally."

"You're joking!" she said.

"Me? I never joke—old serious Hank, they call me."

"No they don't! Inspector Fouchard calls you a mercenary—is that what you are?"

"Depends," Frost said, sighing, "on how you look at it." He offered her a Camel. She refused, then he lit one for himself.

"You're amazing—you're perfectly content with yourself, aren't you?"

"No—that's not true," Frost answered, "but I'm not much upset about myself, either. You really want to know what I'd do if I didn't need money? Well, the Omega's fine and I've got all the spare magazines for my pistol that I can carry. And I don't like wearing suits. There's a girl I know," he went on, thinking of Bess, "and I'd probably marry her. Get myself a little place in northeast Georgia or maybe New Mexico, do some hunting and fishing—maybe write a book. Cull the stuff from my real life experiences as a mercenary—like you call me. Then I could just sit back and watch all the political extremists and crackpots blow themselves up, watch the multi-colored nuclear sunsets or at the best watch my bank balance go up and my buying power go down—stuff like that —whatever."

"There's only one thing I want—my father back," she said, her voice quiet. "I'll get you in with his colleagues, but will that do any good?"

"Only thing I see," Frost said, stubbing out his cigarette, "is to get up the ransom, pay it and try following it back to your father before they count it and kill him. And that's no lead pipe cinch. If a better plan comes along in the meantime, I'll try it."

"You don't offer much encouragement."

"You want encouragement, see a computer dating counselor or something. I thought you wanted the truth."

"Take me back to my hotel now, please," she said, glancing down at the gold lady's Rolex on her wrist. "I've been up all day and I'm very tired. I know we'll want an early start tomorrow."

Frost paid the bill with a credit card—"My God, they gotta be kidding," he muttered, grateful immediately for his expense account.

Sheila took his arm as they left the restaurant. There was no taxi in sight and they started to walk. As they passed an alley – the night particularly dark because the sky was overcast and the street light nearest them out, Frost started getting an uncomfortable feeling.

"Do you hear something?" he whispered to the girl beside him, his right hand clasped to the book with the gun inside it.

"No – what is it, Hank?" Frost heard the sound again, a rapid shuffling of feet across pavement. Pushing the girl away from him he got the little .32 auto out of the book and turned. Three men, at least, were racing toward him from the shadows of the alley. Frost pulled the trigger. The gun fired once and jammed. Though still in shadow, he could see one of the three attackers doubling up and going down, but before Frost could clear the pistol's jam, the other two men were on him. With the heel of his left hand, Frost straight-armed the nearest man in the face, knocking him aside. Wheeling, Frost fell back under a glancing blow from the second man's fist. As the man closed toward him, Frost – his jaw aching – lashed out with his right foot, catching his attacker in the stomach, then moved into a wheeling fighting stance, his left knee smashing into the second man's chin, his right elbow hammering into the side of the man's face as his head raised from the impact of the knee smash.

As the second attacker fell away, Frost turned. The first man was on his feet again and coming toward him. Frost shouted to the girl, "Get out of here!" then backstepped away from his attacker. The man was crouched in a classic martial arts stance, hands moving in the somewhat stylized movement of Gung Fu. The man half-wheeled and went into a flying kick, Frost sidestepping and turning, lashing out with his left foot and catching the man near the tail bone and throwing him off balance. Foolishly, Frost thought, the man tried a flying kick again. This time, Frost feigned sidestepping and going into another wheeling kick, but instead lashed out with his hands. He caught the man's ankle in both his own hands and wrenched it up and to the side. The attacker crashed down to the pavement.

Instinctively, Frost knew better than to go in with his feet. Backing away, the attacker was on his own feet again in an instant, his right fist flashing upward toward Frost's face. No time, Frost thought, backing off, the first kick missing him, a second kick from the opposite foot already coming toward him. With the flat of his left forearm, painfully Frost deflected the blow; then, stepping in toward his attacker, delivered a short jab to the man's face with the heel of his right hand. Half-wheeling, Frost slammed up with the instep of his left foot, impacting against the man's groin, his right elbow missing the man's Adam's apple and connecting with the chest. Frost had misjudged his attacker's height, he realized. As the man fell back, Frost could see from the corner of his eye that the first attacker was on his feet again and coming toward him, but slowly — and evidently in pain. Frost feigned a flying kick toward the second attacker, then wheeled on the still injured first man, his right foot going into a perfect shot at the man's neck. Frost started to turn, the second man coming for him. Out of the corner of his eye, he saw a flash, heard what sounded

73

then like a silenced shot, felt a tingling sensation in the right side of his neck.

Automatically, his right hand reached up toward the impact point of the wound – a dart, he thought. He pulled it out. The second man was coming at him and Frost started to react – but it was as though, Frost thought, his attacker was moving at normal speed and he was moving in slow motion. Unable to get his feet going, Frost started raising his right arm to deflect the force of the kick coming toward his face. His arm was raising, but so slowly, he thought. The pain – he knew there had to be pain – just didn't seem to bother him. As Frost tried turning his head, his left cheek felt terribly stiff. "I can't smile," he thought. The thought itself amused him and Frost started to laugh as the second attacker's fist came toward his face . . .

"Captain Frost? Can you hear me?"

Frost opened his eye. "They won, right?"

"Thank God you're all right," Sheila whispered, breathless sounding. Frost opened his eye again. They were in what looked like some sort of cellar, but finished as a large room. He put his hands down to get himself up to his feet, then looked down beneath his fingers. The floor was hardwood, well finished and freshly waxed. There were two fluorescent tubes glowing in the ceiling of the long, narrow room, and by the comparatively bright light he could see the door at the far end – the steel kind with bands of rivets squaring off the edges.

"You try the door?" Frost asked, testing his

74

legs and seeing if everything worked.

"It's locked. Oh, your poor face – that bruise," and she touched her hand to his left cheek. It hadn't hurt, he thought, until she'd touched it.

He muttered thanks and – stiffly – strode toward the door. He reached it, tried budging it, then turned back toward her, standing behind him. "You were right – sure is locked."

"What will we do, Captain Frost?"

Frost looked at her a moment, noticed the dirt on her face, the tears in her dress – the shawl was gone and so was one earring. "Take off your other earring," he said.

"Can you use it to pick the lock?" she asked, her hands going to her right ear lobe for a second, then handing him the earring.

"No – you keep it," Frost said. "You just looked silly wearing only one earring."

Instinctively, he felt his pockets. Everything was there, including the small pen knife, his wallet with the razor blade and his cigarettes and lighter.

"Could we burn our way out?" she asked, her voice hopeful sounding.

"No," Frost said, "but we could set the floor on fire and suffocate before they discovered it." He scanned the walls – not a window nor any sign of any other way in or out. "They look like Nazis to you?" he asked, exhaling a cloud of gray smoke.

"I don't know – some of them spoke with accents."

"That's a sure sign," Frost said, nodding his head and forcing a smile. When he smiled his head hurt. She was shivering, her shoulders barer than they should have been with the dress ripped. Putting his arm around her, Frost said in a low voice, "Look, if they wanted to kill us right away they would have done it already—let's see what happens." 'Let's see what happens' he repeated to himself. Didn't have much choice, he thought.

"Would you turn your back—I have to pee," she said, gesturing with her right hand toward the far end of the basement and a gleaming looking flush toilet.

Shrugging, Frost said, "Sure," then turned and stared at the door while he listened to the click of her heels against the floor, heard her working the toilet paper roll, heard the "tinkling" sound, then the sound of the chain being pulled.

"You can turn around now," she called and Frost turned around. She was sidestepping, embarrassed looking, away from the toilet. Then, stopping, she said, "What are we going to do?"

Frost looked at her a moment, then outstretching his hand and touching her left shoulder with his fingers, said, "We've got nothing we can do—not until they come for us anyway. You're still cold?"

"Yes," she said, quietly, barely audible, then moving hesitantly closer to him.

"Lie down with me then," Frost whispered, then took her in his arms. To Frost, there seemed to be no spot of floor that looked more appealing or comfortable than any other, so he dropped to his knees there and brought her down beside him, his hands gently touching at her bare shoulder, then his fingers slowly moving down to her breasts.

He touched his lips to her neck and she leaned her head back, a soft, almost purring sound coming from her. There was more of the renegade hair now at the nape of her neck, and Frost ran his fingers up the long, gracefully curving throat and with his right hand fumbled the pins away and loosened her dark hair. "Perfume?" he whispered.

"Uh-huh," she answered.

He kissed her neck, entwining the fingers of his right hand in her hair and cocking her head back. Her lips—the lipstick all but gone—were a' cherry color, like cherries just ripening. Moist tasting against his own, he kissed her, their tongues touching. He cradled her in his left arm, his right hand against her face, then drifting down across her body, brushing against the thin fabric still but barely covering her breasts, moving inexorably downward. His hand slid up under her dress and his fingers could feel the heat of her through the panties she wore.

Roughly, he pulled them down, and then the pantyhose, his fingers probing inside her at the moist triangle of hair at her crotch. He brought her down to the floor with him, then undid his belt and opened his pants, pushing them down. He could hear in the background the sound of her kicking away her shoes.

Pulling her panties down all the way, and then the stockings, he bunched the skirt of her dress and her slip up toward her waist, sliding his body between her legs. By comparison to the cold of the floor and the fear Frost judged was in both their hearts, the heat from her thighs pressed against him was unimaginably warm.

77

Already, he could feel himself erect, her fingers, gently at first and then almost demandingly, touching him there. He started to come inside her, felt her, heard her wince, then withdrew. With his fingers, he rubbed her and after a few moments as he kissed her, he took his fingers away, moist. This time when he started inside her she moaned a heavy sigh and wrapped her arms around him, her lips brushing against his cheek . . .

Chapter Seven

"About time you guys got here—I'm almost out of cigarettes," Frost cracked, sitting cross-legged on the floor in the middle of the room, Sheila curled up beside him. The black face of the Omega on his wrist read 7:00 A. M. As the four men started toward him, one limping slightly in the left leg —Frost pegged him as the man who'd shot the dart into his neck back in the alley—Frost, his coat covering the girl's shoulders, started pushing his shirt sleeves down, then started to get up.

"Try nothing funny," the man who was limping said.

"How about a joke to brighten things up?" Frost asked, reaching his feet and squaring off as the four—seemingly unarmed—approached him.

"You both will come with us, Captain Frost."

"Oh—sure," Frost said. The limping man was close to him now and Frost lashed out with his right hand, a back hand swipe, the razor blade tucked between the second and third fingers and braced there with one of the toothpicks. As his hand shot forward, the limping man tried backing off, but was too slow. Frost's right, the smallest edge of the razor blade barely protruding between the fingers, connected, the tip of its edge catching in the flesh of the limping man's left cheek, then ripping. As the man's face started gushing blood at the spot, Frost's hand finished its swing.

Frost took a step back, the other three men coming toward him. The limping man was screaming, a crimson line almost bisecting the lower half of his face, blood streaming from it.

As the closest of the other three started toward him, Frost's left hand whipped the belt from around his waist. Swinging it, he curled the belt twice around his left fist, the buckle moving like a flail. "Come on, guys," Frost snarled. As the first of the remaining three started for him, he sidestepped and swung the belt, the heavy trophy buckle crashing down hard against the side of the man's head. Frost wheeled, slapping backhand with his razor blade armed right fist, his target the second of the three remaining men. The man threw up his right arm, blocking Frost's blow toward his face. As Frost wheeled, then started countering with the belt, he could see the white shirt sleeve of the man's

80

right arm starting to soak through with blood.

His belt buckle connected, a glancing blow to the second man's left temple. The third of the remaining three was diving toward Frost now, and he couldn't get out of his way. The man's head slammed into his stomach and both men went down. "Football!" The word flashed through Frost's mind.

Rolling out from under the man, he drew his right back and hammered it forward, his fist jabbing square on into the man's jaw and knocking him down. Frost hauled himself to his feet, shaking his right fist. The razor blade was gone somewhere, he discovered, and he half thought he might have broken his hand against the last man's jaw. Grabbing the girl's hand, Frost started for the door. The first man, whom Frost had slashed in the face, was on his knees, his hands in front of his eyes. As Frost started past the man he'd disabled with the belt buckle, he could see him starting to get up. Half-turning, Frost kicked him in the side of the head, once, then again.

Holding the girl's right hand in his left, the belt still held like a flail but in his right hand now, Frost reached the doorway — then stopped.

"You are a most formidable fighter, Captain Frost." The voice was perfect Midwestern American English, the face was deeply tanned and clean shaven, the submachine gun in the hands was an Uzi. "I too am a Captain — Yuri Karkov; I am with the Mossad — you know the name?"

"If I answer correctly," Frost said, breathless, "and say Israeli Intelligence, do I get five hundred dollars and move onto the next square?"

81

"Try five thousand dollars, Captain Frost — and best of all, you get to live — "

In sharp contrast to the cold and empty cellar, Frost thought, the dining room where they sat now, sunlight streaming in through the sheer white curtains on the eight-foot windows, was pleasant — exceedingly so. A young woman had brought them breakfast of fresh rolls — Danish, Frost called them — and coffee. Frost leaned back, lighting a cigarette from a fresh pack of Camels they'd provided him with as the girl sat down at the table and joined them. Now there were four at the table — Frost, Sheila Balsam, Captain Karkov and the girl — he thought he remembered her name as Miriam something.

"My men are not happy with you, Captain."

"I wasn't too happy with them, Captain," Frost said through a cloud of smoke. Leaning forward he sipped at his second cup of coffee. "Why the routine in the alley, then, last night — what do you want?"

"We want you — to help us and at the same time move closer toward rescuing Dr. Balsam."

"For that you try mugging me, shoot me up with a drugged dart and get four of your men put in the hospital — I assume that's where they are."

"A field hospital, so to speak, but yes — we share one here with the CIA. They don't ask us questions and we don't ask them questions. Works very nicely. Beautiful old building — be careful you don't get to see it." Karkov took another carrot stick and chewed on it. He drank no coffee, had disdained the rolls and was working on a second glass of milk.

"You're into health food, right?"

"In a manner of speaking," Karkov said, smiling. "Will you help us?"

"Why the rough stuff—answer me first."

"Very simple—we didn't wish to hire a man who couldn't take care of the job we have in mind. So congratulations—you passed our test—with flying colors."

Frost smiled. "I bet those four guys aren't happy about it."

"Right again, Captain," Karkov said. "You are a brutal man—but then ours is a brutal business, isn't it?"

"Got me," Frost said, shaking his head. Then, "But just exactly what's this little job you've got in mind?"

"And how will it help to find my father?" Sheila Balsam interjected.

"I want you to infiltrate the French neo-Nazi movement for us—not nearly as difficult as it might sound, especially to a man with your skills. There is a certain American, a member of the Nazi party. His name is James William Carlson—J. W. is what he goes by. Like you, he was blinded in his left eye, wears an eyepatch. Otherwise, you are physically similar. A change of hairstyles, shaving off the mustache you wear, different clothes, a different watch, a gun like the one he always carries and it should be perfectly believable."

"I don't change watches," Frost said, a smile crossing his lips. Then turning to avoid the sunlight in his eye, he lit another cigarette.

"Do you always wear that watch on your wrist?" Sheila Balsam asked.

"Well," Frost said, "back in the days of my military training—which has proven of fundamental value to me in my civilian life too, let me tell ya'—I always used to wear the watch on my neck. I had a special face made for it, in reverse and I carried this pocket mirror. Whenever I wanted to know what time it was, I just held that little mirror up in front of my throat and read my watch. But then after I lost my left eye—I'm far-sighted in the right eye—I started developing eye strain and got an extension handle for the mirror so I could read my watch from farther away, but that made me begin to feel self-conscious, so now I wear it on my wrist."

"You amaze me, Captain Frost—why aren't you a joke writer for a nightclub entertainer?"

Smiling, Frost said, "Hey—that's a wonderful idea," then, rising half-out of his seat, said, "well, see you guys—let me know how the war goes and everything."

As Karkov started to get up, Frost dropped back into his seat and groaned, "Relax—too serious, that's what you are."

"Will you try to infiltrate the French Nazi party as J. W. Carlson?" Karkov leaned forward, peering intently, Frost thought, toward him.

"Gotta shave the mustache, too, huh? Hmm . . . " Glancing at the girl, Frost looked back to Karkov, saying, "Let me have another cup of coffee first, though, huh?"

Frost shaved the mustache with more than a

little remorse, he felt. After more than ten years wearing one, to him its removal was no less casual than temporarily removing – an eye. As he stared at himself in the bathroom mirror, he wished the eye were indeed temporary. His hair had already been trimmed – the girl called Miriam had turned out to be a not-bad barber. His sideburns were nearly gone and she'd trimmed the sides of his hair to accentuate the touch of grey already there – J. W. Carlson was five years older than Frost, making Carlson nearly forty.

Splashing water on his face to rinse away the loose hairs, Frost dried his skin and replaced his eyepatch. Before leaving the bathroom, he decided to urinate, then washed his hands and left, rejoining Captain Karkov and Sheila Balsam in the dining room. The sun was setting now, the day spent in memorizing the few details there were that seemed necessary to J. W. Carlson's identity – memorizing a man's entire past in a single day was impossible.

Carlson was wanted in the United States for suspicion of first degree murder, conspiracy, interstate flight to avoid prosecution, grand theft auto and assaulting a police officer. Like Frost, Carlson was a veteran of Viet Nam, but unlike Frost also a veteran of Fort Levenworth. Carlson had apparently joined the American Nazi Party in his youth on Chicago's South Side, been involved with the white power demonstrations when Dr. King had led open housing marches there not long before his death. Carlson's left eye had been lost in a small race riot – he'd apparently started it – in a county jail in Arkansas. Escaping from the hospital, he'd started his latest wave of mayhem for which he was now wanted by the FBI.

Sitting down opposite Karkov, Frost gestured to his naked upper lip and asked, "Now what, chief?"

"The gun, and a few last minute directions. No matter what, Carlson always carries one of these— we took this gun from him when we incarcerated him." As Karkov reached into the battered brief-case on the table beside him, Frost said, "You never told me—just where is this guy?"

"In Israel, in a military hospital, under heavy sedation—he was trying to join the PLO and some-one from our civilian police force spotted him from the wanted notices the FBI had circulated through Interpol when they suspected Carlson had left your country. This is his gun."

Karkov drew a holster-worn Colt Gold Cup National Match .45 from the case, along with a crudely made inside-the-pants holster. "Talk about things that don't go together—your guys check the springs on this, that it holds up with full house loads— I've never used a Gold Cup. Some people say it's just for target loads."

"I wouldn't know about all of these, Captain Frost, but this one checked out with the ammo Carlson was using—185-grain jacketed hollow points, if I remember correctly."

Karkov slid the gun across the table, then three scratched-up magazines and a box of cartridges. Frost checked the magazine release, the slide stop, the functioning of the grip safety—it was impossi-ble to check the adjustable rear sight without going to a range and firing. He looked back to Karkov as he loaded the three magazines, then said, "Does this guy carry with seven or eight rounds – do you know?"

"What do you mean?" Karkov said.

"Well, a lot of professional gunmen insist that it's better to forego the extra round in the chamber and just simply load the chambered round straight out of the top of the magazine – edges the next round slightly forward and makes for smoother feeding – I do that a lot of times myself."

"I have nothing in my notes about that," Karkov said, sounding, Frost thought, a little out of his depth.

Ramming the magazine up the butt of the .45, Frost jacked back the slide and ran it forward. "Well, we'll say he's professional," he said, then cautiously let the hammer down, sliding the pistol into his belt. "You can keep the holster – here."

"But –"

Frost put the loaded spare magazines into his breast pocket, then pocketed a handful of loose rounds as well, saying, "Just tell the Nazis I lost the holster. I wouldn't wear that thing if you paid me – even though you are paying me. Now where do I go?"

The instructions were simple enough, and before he walked through the doors and into the dark outside, Karkov arranged for Sheila, who would be taken home separately, to be Frost's contact. She could not be known as a member of Mossad, since she was not, and it was unlikely she would be recognized as Balsam's daughter. Frost wasn't particularly happy with the idea, but acquiesced.

Once on the street — a suburban community outside Paris, he'd been told — he walked in the direction he had been pointed, toward the Metro station. Karkov had given him a ticket, Miriam had given him a smile, and Sheila had given him a kiss. And Karkov had also given him a code phrase.

He left the train he took into the city, then boarded another line and traveled three stops, then left the Metro. As Frost walked down the sparsely traveled street, he reflected that the area was quite different from the suburb where Israeli intelligence had its headquarters. Like most large cities, Frost was learning, Paris had its fair share of good and bad spots — and this street was somewhere in the middle. Not the sort of place where you'd stand around counting hundred dollar bills on the street corner, but not a mugger's paradise either.

The clock shop — his destination — was visible as he rounded the corner, heading he surmised, north. Within sight of the picture window at the front of the shop, he stopped, being obvious in case anyone was watching as he removed the Seiko on his wrist, then deliberately twisted the expansion band to bend the links out of shape. Dropping the watch into his pocket, he snapped up the collar of the stained raincoat he wore, pulled the tyrolean hat down over his face and walked on. It was starting to rain.

Frost stopped at the foot of the three steps leading up to the clock shop entrance. The shop looked closed, but there was a small light burning in the rear. He went up the steps and knocked on the tan-curtained glass door. He knocked again. He heard something through the glass—in French, he suspected. But in English Frost shouted, the first portion of the code phrase, "My watch is something I rely on—the band is broken."

The shouting from inside stopped and Frost saw another, larger light going on, the edges of the curtain in the door glowing yellow now with its brightness. As the curtain was drawn back slightly, he saw a man's face; then the door opened on a crack, still secured with a chain guard.

"What is it that you want?" the man asked, his accent not quite right, but the English good enough.

Frost repeated the code phrase, "My watch is something I rely on—the band is broken."

The older man said, "But if it is only the band, I cannot see where it is unusable. Perhaps tomorrow."

"But I must leave tonight," Frost answered. There was no more of the code phrase, so Frost waited. After a long minute, the man, his voice changing slightly, the German accent to his English more apparent now, said, "Come in out of the rain."

As Frost came up the last step and started past the door, he wondered if it was more like out of the frying pan—and into the fire.

Chapter Eight

"This is Genevieve," the old man said, then left through the curtain through which he and Frost had just passed seconds earlier, entering from the main portion of the clock shop into the smaller back room.

Frost extended his right hand to the woman sitting at the small table, various parts of time-piece mechanisms ranked in orderly fashion before her, a jeweler's eyepiece in place on her left eye. She was blond-haired, forty or so, Frost guessed, and anything more than that was impossible to tell.

After a long silence, his hand ignored, the woman looked up, dropping the eyepiece into her hand. Her eyes were bright blue, at least so they seemed to Frost in the yellow light of the lamp at the head of the table where she worked. "As he told you, I am Genevieve. I seem to know your face."

Frost forced a look of discomfort, then said, "Are you with the—"

"Who are you, first?"

"J. W. Carlson—you can just call me J. W., though. Miss . . . ?"

"Genevieve will do for now."

Smiling, Frost said. "Well, Miss Wildufernau, it's a pleasure to meet you."

The woman's face never cracked. Throwing up his hands, Frost sat against the edge of the table, then said, "Look—let's cut the crap. You know who I am if you recognize the face and this," and Frost gestured to the eyepatch. "Are you the contact from the Party. If I got the wrong clock shop, I'll leave."

"Do you expect me to greet you with 'Heil Hitler'? I should hardly think so. You are still a wanted man, as I recall, Mr. Carlson. And how do I know you are you—who you say you are?"

"Well," Frost said, his hand appearing from under his raincoat with the Gold Cup tight in his fist, the sound of the hammer raising to full stand under his thumb like the sound of a bomb dropping in the otherwise stillness, the mechanical hums of the clocks in the background barely audible. "Just a yes or no, lady—otherwise—" Frost gestured with the nearly half-inch diameter muzzle of the pistol.

"Yes—you are J. W. Carlson. Sources indicated you were in North Africa—in Palestine."

"Them Jew cops are pretty tough," Frost replied, trying to keep the remark in Carlson's character.

"But not for long, hmmm?" she almost purred. "I will introduce you to the Party leadership here —as you know, we are controlled by headquarters and function with the local Party regulars but are not part of their organization. I can get you well connected, as I think the Americanism goes."

"Wonderful," Frost said, emotionless.

"But we can get connected in still another way while we wait until I can introduce you—you should appreciate a pun like that. I have read a great deal about your work in the Party in America. You are a fine assassin, J. W."

"Well," Frost grunted noncommittally. He didn't know Carlson was actually an assassin and he wasn't about to get drawn into a conversation along that line.

"We can make love while we wait, no?"

Frost didn't quite know what to say, but gambled, saying "If you like—I been on the road a lot, kind of tired."

"I can awaken you, J. W.," Genevieve said.

Frost shrugged, made the Gold Cup disappear inside the waistband of his trousers, then remarked, "Lost my holster a ways back, gotta get a new one or make one."

Genevieve stood up, then moved toward him. "We can go to my place. It isn't far." For the first time, Frost could actually see her. The blond hair was full and beautiful, the eyes were blue—very. Her figure looked well endowed under the knit dress she wore. Shrugging his shoulders again, Frost said, "Why, not, kid."

Her apartment was a block and a half away, the building appearing dingy but the second floor apartment Genevieve occupied pleasant and well lit — more appropriately flooded with light, Frost thought — as she flicked the wall switch.

"Sit down — what would you like to drink, J. W.?"

Frost was ready for that. Almost grimacing, he said, "If you don't have rye, I'll take some bourbon — straight up."

The woman smiled and disappeared into what Frost assumed was the kitchen. Dropping his now sodden raincoat across a wooden dining room chair, he sank down into the couch and lit a cigarette — Carlson smoked Kools. The thought amused Frost as he inhaled the menthol tasting smoke. Carlson was known not only for hating Jews, but also for hating blacks — to Frost's reckoning, a disproportionately large number of blacks smoked menthol cigarettes, as he recalled. Frost flipped his Zippo in his hand, pocketing it as the woman returned — Carlson carried a Zippo, too.

"Here, J. W. — I didn't have rye. But this is good bourbon."

"Thanks, kid," Frost said, sipping at the drink. He hated bourbon.

"Come into my bedroom, you can finish your drink there."

Hauling himself out of the low couch, Frost pulled his tie down past half mast and followed her.

There was a stereo in the corner of the room and she went to it and put a record on — Charles

Aznavour. Frost looked at her, saying "Shut that thing off, will you?" He'd listened to Aznavour last when he was with Bess in Switzerland, and he had no desire to spoil a pleasant memory with what was going to happen.

She clicked off the stereo and walked over toward the bed, the only light in the room now a small lamp beside it. "Undress me," she said.

Frost walked toward her and she came into his arms. He felt behind her, found a zipper and tugged at it, then remembered to search with his fingers for the hook at the top of the neckline. He undid it. She took her arms from around his neck and shrugged, the dress falling down around her ankles. She wasn't wearing a bra, as Frost had guessed when she'd first stood up in front of him back at the clock shop. No stockings either, he noticed, just a too-short white slip and panties. He pushed these down past her hips. She dropped two inches in front of him as she kicked away her shoes. He took her in his arms and holding her left breast in his right hand, curled his left arm around behind her, his fingers knotting in the hair that cascaded past her shoulders, his mouth now centimeters from hers.

He watched her eyes a moment before he kissed her, heard her whisper, "Do one-eyed men kiss better?"

"That's not all they do better, kid," he whispered back, then drew her face to him, his mouth going down on hers . . .

He lay back on the bed and felt her hands at his belt, then working his zipper down. "I can undress myself, Genevieve."

94

"I want to," she whispered, and in a moment he felt her mouth against him. Frost sighed heavily, balling his fists into knots, then bent down quickly and drew her up to him. Arching her back, he pulled her beneath him, felt her hands at his penis, the hardness that was involuntary with him now though he didn't even like the woman, knew what and who she was, would have shot her given half the chance.

"Violence . . . " The word flashed across his mind. And that's all this is, he thought. Not love, not even sex — violence. And violently then he pushed his way into her and she dug her nails into his back and into his rear end, her breathing heavy. He thought he heard her rasp the word, "Again," as he sank against her.

He dressed while she showered, checked his gun that she had not tampered with it and perfunctorily smoked another of the menthol cigarettes while she dressed. She had a small car — a Renault — and he drove with her across town to a neighborhood that looked far worse than the area where the clock shop had been. The major occupation of everyone seemed to be related there to the clubs which dotted the street. As they left the car near an alley and walked a block toward the main avenue, Frost spotted at least a half-dozen hookers, both male and female.

"Looks like a nice place," Frost cracked as she tugged at his elbow, guiding him toward the second doorway from the corner. The marquee read "Gay Paris" and he realized what it meant when they went inside. At a quick glance, Frost judged a good twenty-five percent of the patrons were in drag, which, he figured, meant probably double that and he just couldn't tell. There was a red-haired "woman" with black hair on her back who guided Genevieve – whom "she" apparently knew – and Frost to a back corner table, still only five yards from the dance floor.

Frost ordered a bourbon from the "waitress" and Genevieve ordered gin. "You want to dance?" Genevieve asked. Frost remembered vaguely that Carlson considered himself a good dancer.

"Sure," Frost said. The music was disco, loud and off records rather than a live orchestra. When their drinks came, Frost belted his half away, the bourbon burning his throat, and followed her – already up – out onto the floor. There was what Frost labelled a 1920s dance hall prism rotating over the floor, reflecting every small table light and spotlight in the place. One record died away, and as it did another cut in – a disco version of something Frost vaguely identified as Beethoven.

As Genevieve started undulating across from him, Frost shrugged and said mentally "What the hell?" and decided to do it right. His right arm shot up and out and he started to dance.

"All right!" she shouted excitedly. Frost drew her into his arms and snapped her away. She turned toward him and moved beside him. The floor was crowded and hot now, and as Frost looked around he could see that roughly half the couples on the floor were heterosexual – the others weren't. He started to laugh.

"What is it?" she shouted over the music.

"Nothing," he shouted back, answering loud

so she could hear, then laughing still louder. Hank Frost — getting down and boogeying in a gay bar, he thought. "If Bess could see me now!" he almost verbalized.

The song ended and the next was slower, the group familiar to him — American — but he couldn't recall the name. There was almost a tango rhythm to it, and Frost brought Genevieve into his arms, guiding her across the floor, dipping her and then taking her back across the floor. He heard her loud stage whisper in his ear, "You are a fantastic dancer, J. W."

"Like I said, one-eyed men do it better, kid," Frost answered, laughing as he drew her to him, then spun her away, then brought her back into his arms.

This song ended too, and as a loud pre-recorded drum roll sounded Frost turned toward the center of the floor, Genevieve whispered, "The show — it is starting."

He nodded, then taking her elbow and moving back toward their table, added, "I can hardly wait."

As the show got under way, Frost decided he *should* have waited. It was a crudely choreographed SM routine. He decided too that he could have done a better job of staging the numbers himself. The costumes were black leather that looked more like vinyl, the whips, the chains — everything seemed a little old, including the bosomy-looking blond-wigged man who was writhing across the stage with a cat-o-nine-tails in hand, swinging away at a thin, intentionally effeminate looking man chained to a tin-plated grillwork in the center of what had been the dance floor.

As Frost watched the audience, though, he decided his "review" wasn't an accurate reflection of public taste. Both the straights and the gays in the darkened audience – from what he could make out of their facial expressions – were enjoying themselves and wildly applauding, hooting, whistling. Frost turned suddenly, startled at a loud whistle Genevieve had made.

He leaned back and finished his bourbon as the effeminate looking "whippee" started crawling on his knees toward the "whipper," the whippee's tongue hanging out.

Frost leaned toward Genevieve, loud-whispering in her ear, "Is he gonna . . . ?"

"Uh-huh," she said, hardly glancing at him, her voice breathless, her eyes rivetted to the floor.

"My goodness," Frost said, half to himself, "my mommy never took me anyplace like this." As the effeminate looking boy finally crawled toward the guy in drag who was holding the whip and started to do what Frost had guessed, he lit one of his cigarettes, muttering, "My goodness!"

As the show dragged on, he realized that what had first shocked him was mild, and as the show ended, screams and applause erupting like a shockwave around him, Frost turned back and looked at Genevieve. "They do this every night?" he asked.

"*Oui,* but this is the last show tonight – the club will close in a while."

"Ohh," he said, just nodding his head.

"In a few minutes," she said, "I will take you

back stage and you can meet your contact."

Frost forced a smile and flagged over the "waitress" and ordered another bourbon and another gin for the girl. The music started again and some of the couples—but the crowd was thinning out—started back onto the floor. Genevieve looked at him, but Frost said, "Naw—let's sit this one out, kid."

He checked the watch in his pocket—the woman had never fixed the band—and saw that it was nearly 4:00 A.M.

By the time Frost finished the bourbon and Genevieve had finished her gin, she said, "Come along—J. W. I will introduce you."

Standing, he followed her through the forest of tables and back through a ragged looking beaded curtain—backstage. There was one door on each side of the hall, the one on his right sounding as though there were a party on the other side. "That is for the chorus," she said. She knocked on the door on the left. "This is his dressing room," she said, her voice sounding almost awed.

"*Entre*," was all Frost heard and he followed Genevieve inside. It looked to Frost like a typical movie version of a dressing room in a cheap theater, and the man behind the dressing table, taking off his make-up, was the bosomy blond with the whip.

"This is J. W. Carlson, Victor, J. W.," Genevieve said, "this is Victor Liebling, the Commander of the Paris division of the French National Socialist Workers Party."

Victor Liebling turned toward Frost and extended his hand. Frost took it. And as soon as he did, Frost realized he'd been suckered by an old west gun-slinger trick. Liebling—amazingly strong—dragged Frost's right hand forward. As Frost started with his left hand for the gun carried butt forward behind his left hip bone, he felt something sharp at his back, Pain, heat. A knife? The thought flashed across his mind, but suddenly Frost fell forward to his knees.

"Can you hear me—Herr Carlson?"

Frost could barely speak—all he could see were wildly changing colors; his ears were ringing. "You've merely been drugged. Don't be distressed. We checked your fingerprints on the glass from Genevieve's house—the Sûreté shows they do not belong to J. W. Carlson. That means that—since you are not who you say you are—you must be working for the CIA or the Israeli Mossad. But you are not Carlson."

Frost looked up at the grotesquely half-madeup face, trying to say something, but his tongue too thick to work, his lips numb, his throat tight.

"Mustn't try to talk, Herr whoever you are. But we will find out."

Frost tried to speak again.

"Ohh," Liebling almost cooed, "you want to know how we knew. Very simple—I'll call you Carlson for now. Very simple. After your evening with Genevieve we knew—Carlson is an almost fanatical homosexual."

Frost closed his eye, trying to verbalize the word, "Oops!"

Chapter Nine

Frost opened his eye, then closed it again, squeezing the muscles around it tightly to focus, then trying to see once again. He was cold, and as he looked down he saw that he was naked, his arms suspended – he looked up – from a hook on a rafter in what appeared to be a large room in an old country house. His feet were high off the floor. He looked up again – handcuffs were locked to his wrists, but the cuffs were wide like antique manacles, the chain links like automobile chain in its thickness. The room, he decided, was apparently a library, three of the four walls lined with books; a roaring hearth blazing in the center of the fourth wall, the massive mantel flagstone.

But interspersed with the bookcases, Frost saw,

101

were a wide assortment of things somewhat recognized, although he didn't know—nor care to know—the names. As he stared at the objects, the thought crossed his mind that perhaps all humans recognized these things—that they were part of the human racial subconscious—the terror they inspired. There were barbed shackles, separated by what looked to be adjustable iron bars, collars with massive screws at the sides, wooden blocks that tightened like a vice, half-opened hinged masks with tiny spikes lining the inside. He spied a pair of what looked like cast iron boots, grillwork where the soles of normal boots would have been. Hot coals went there, he surmised.

"Interesting—I see you've noticed the decorations, Herr Carlson. Before we begin the evening's entertainment, would you care to tell us your real name?" It was Liebling who had spoken and Frost turned his head to look down toward him. Beside Liebling sat several other men—faces he recognized from the floor-show. The only woman was Genevieve. The leather chairs were lined up in a semi-circle just out of reach of Frost's feet if he were to kick. Indeed, Frost thought, they looked as though they were ready and waiting for a show.

"Your name!" Liebling shouted.

Frost glared at him, then quietly said, "Go to hell, wimp!"

Seemingly undisturbed at the remark, Liebling droned, "There are three questions I wish answered—and we will make you answer them in what will be to ourselves a quite enjoyable manner. First, who are you and who do you work for; next, why have you tried to infiltrate our organization and how much is known to your organization about us; third, what knowledge do you have of who has really kidnapped this Jew professor, Balsam?"

Frost thought, had he been standing up, he would have fallen over. This was the leader of the Nazis around Paris and he knew nothing of the kidnapping of Doctor Balsam.

"Do you wish to answer us now? You will answer us later. We can and will do things to your body, to your mind, that will make you pray for death."

Frost saw no advantage, he felt, in admitting what he knew, or who he was. And there was no advantage in being polite, either. "Why don't you tell me, 'Ve have vays of making even zee strongest person beg to tell us vat ve vant to know'?"

"You will pay for your tongue. Genevieve — since you brought this nice man to us, you may have him to play with first."

From the corner of his eye, Frost noticed Genevieve standing up, smoothing her skirt down with her hands, then walking out of his line of vision. But in a moment she reappeared on his other side, a straight razor and a strap in her hands. "Your body is too hairy, whoever you are. These scars on your legs — bullet wounds. Perhaps the skin is still more tender there, hmmm? I will start there."

As she stropped the razor, Frost heard the cackling of the Nazis who were watching him. But as soon as she touched the razor to the skin of his legs and began to flail it away, Frost could no longer hear them — he was screaming too loudly . . . He was conscious. Somehow, unconsciousness wouldn't come to him. He could feel the pain, but that was all he could feel or sense. She would work with the razor for a while, cutting away the flesh on his legs, then step away, admiring—evidently—what she had done, then drop the razor in the pocket of her skirt. Methodically, predictably, she would then take the two-inch wide strop—double thick of heavy leather—and beat his legs, over the wounds. The rationale, Frost guessed, was that stimulation of the area would heighten the pain where she had peeled away the skin. It went on, and on, and still he said nothing, screaming with the pain, unable to pass out.

He heard Liebling saying, "All right, Genevieve—you've had enough fun." Then the tone of voice changing, he said to Frost, "And you—have you had enough screaming —will you tell us?"

Frost was in too much pain to even answer, simply nodding his head, "No."

"You know, the tragic thing is that you may know nothing—and by the time we have had our fill, you might not even remember your name. Marcel —you are next, but save enough of him for us all. Genevieve was so greedy."

The laughter began again, the tall, effeminate looking young man from the stage routine rising from his seat, knees together, his walk more feminine than Genevieve's had been. He took short steps, Frost noticed, and the blue jeans he wore—the designer kind—were so tight Frost absently wondered how the man could move.

Marcel, Frost watched, walked toward the fire-place, reached down for a poker that had been resting in the fire and raised it, examining the tip just an inch or so from his face. Frost watched as Marcel walked toward him, then held the white hot tip glowing in front of him. The man said nothing, but then, his gleaming white teeth bared in a smile, started to walk behind Frost. Frost craned his neck to see—

"No, Marcel, the poker in the rectum could kill him—not yet!"

The voice behind Frost—it was the first time Frost had heard the man named Marcel speak—was a high-pitched scream. "Then I don't want to play—if I cannot do what I want." From the corner of his eye Frost could see Marcel stamping toward the library doors, taking the hot poker and throwing it into the fireplace, then walking out.

Frost had decided that, Nazis or not, the best way to define his tormentors was as being insane. He had gone through torture sessions before. He doubted that anything short of death could cause more pain than when the skin had been peeled away in patches from his legs. As he watched Liebling rising to his feet and coming to stand in front of him, the look in his eyes destroyed Frost's resolve. There could be worse pain—he could read it there.

From a pocket of his suede jacket, Liebling extracted what looked like a half dozen small-in-diameter, long metal corkscrews. "I am going to slowly twist these into your testicles, my silent friend—and then when you beg to die I may let you—after you tell me what I need to know."

Frost felt himself starting to vomit, but held it back. He was already gagging; his arms high over his head were constricting his ribs and breathing was difficult. But Frost said nothing.

As Liebling took the first corkscrew-like skewer and touched its sharp tip to Frost's right testicle, Frost heard a scream—not his own. It sounded like Marcel. There was another voice from behind him, then the sound of running feet. Frost, seeing one of the other Nazis running toward the library doors, noticed for the first time that sun was streaming through a crack in the heavy drapes—it was morning.

The Nazi standing by the doorway was shouting. "Marcel—he has set his room afire again. Come quickly!"

"I shall be back—" Liebling almost spat the words at Frost, dropped the skewers to the floor and ran out through the doorway, shouting, "Genevieve—watch him!"

Frost looked down at his legs, literally raw and bleeding. The plastic tarp protecting the Oriental rug below him was covered with dots of blood, some bright and wet and his own, the other, darker stains, dried, apparently from other hapless victims played with there. Frost looked up and Genevieve was standing a few feet in front of him, a straight razor in her hands again. "He did not say I could not play with you while he was gone, did he? What if I cut away the lid from your other eye—that would be amusing, no?"

She walked to the side of the room and got a small leather covered footstool, picked it up easily in one hand and brought it over in front of him, then stepped up on it. Her eyes were level with his eye now, and she brandished the razor in front of him.

"What is your name?"

Frost looked into her eyes, closed his eye as if passing out with pain, and whispered, "Hank Frost."

"What did you say?"

He opened his eye, smiled and said—"Frost!" Frost lashed out with his right knee, catching the woman in the stomach, knocking her off balance. As she fell, Frost clamped his legs together, catching her about the neck, squeezing them as tightly as he could.

He could hear her screaming, hear himself screaming, the pain in his legs unbearable. He concentrated —"Gotta break her neck" he repeated over and over again. At the back of his mind he knew that he could not escape, but this woman had to die. He twisted his legs together and swung himself on the cuffs, his wrists feeling as though his very hands were ripping away.

There was a short loud scream that never quite came off and Frost looked down. Genevieve's head was between his knees, the eyes wide open, the face slightly purple, the tongue lolling out. As Frost swung himself forward, he let her go and she fell to the floor in front of him, her body bouncing once but not moving after that.

Frost hung there a moment, the exertion making him start to pass out. He looked up, sweat streaming from his forehead and hair despite the fact that he felt terribly cold, his legs and arms trembling, his breathing heavy. He had expected to see the other Nazis running in, having heard the screams—then kill him.

There was smoke streaming through the hallway

107

and starting to filter through the library doors. "The fire," he said. "Still putting out the fire that whacko started."

Frost craned his neck to look up, shaking his head to clear the heavy drops of sweat from his eye. The shackles were suspended—he remembered now—from a hook, the hook screwed or driven in —he couldn't tell which—to the cross beam of the ceiling.

Frost knew what he had to do, and he doubted he'd have the strength to try it once, certainly no more than that. He started his body swinging from the shackles, his wrists dripping blood as he looked up. He forced his hands to move and grasp the chain by which the shackles were attached. The chain started slipping, his right wrist drawn up, his left wrist lower down. He stretched the fingers of his right hand. Barely, he could touch the edge of the beam, and he left his fingers there as he continued his swing.

The arc his feet made compared to the ground was a little greater with each swing. He arched his back, then drew himself forward, the pain in his back almost forcing him down into unconsciousness. But now the arc was greater, his swings taking him farther. A little more, he thought. A little more. Arching his back as though for a dive from a platform, or like a child on a swing, he jacknifed his legs forward and up, the force of the swing carrying him. He hooked one ankle over the beam, the other slipping. Forcing himself, the pain now an all-consuming dulling of his reflexes, he pushed the other ankle up, then worked his bleeding legs up

108

onto and over the beam. Locking his legs together, he wrenched against the chain – the chain came away from the hook and he swung down, suspended by his legs. There was nothing to do, he knew, but let go.

He went down hard, darkness starting to wash over him, his fingers biting into the bloody plastic tarp under him, the message in his brain saying "sleep," the message his dust dry mouth kept mumbling, "Stay awake."

He rolled over onto his back, the pain subsiding a moment and his mind now fighting back the unconsciousness. To keep from passing out, slowly, Frost got himself to his knees. He was trembling, freezing, sweating, his legs crimson with his own blood.

He knelt there a moment, the thought nagging at the back of his mind that the Nazi torturers had to be coming back by now. The smoke in the hallway was starting to clear. Frost couldn't stand, so he crawled across the room – Genevieve had had a shoulder bag when they'd gone to the club and he thought somehow that he'd remembered seeing it beside her chair there in the library.

He spotted it and crawled toward it. He found the bag. Inside it was a Hershey bar. He ripped the paper away from it and bit off a chunk – sugar. His body needed that. There was a gun – one of the best of its type ever made, he thought, but the caliber nothing to enthuse about – a Browning Baby Model .25 automatic – the ladies' version with the pearl plastic grips, the alloy frame and the nickel plate finish.

He checked the chamber, verifying that the protruding loaded chamber indicator was working. One round chambered, six in the magazine. He found no spares. Perfunctorily, his hands moving almost independently of his mind, he checked her purse for a key—nothing. Frost finished the chocolate bar, and as he started to stand up he almost vomited, but kept it down. With the loss of blood, sugar was something he needed desperately, he knew.

Frost tried standing again, then lurched toward the door. Still naked, he was barely conscious of it. At the door, he saw the fire still raging upstairs, heard the angry shouts of the other Nazis, the simpering screams of Marcel. "Marcel—you are gonna die, man," Frost muttered. Something inside him told him that he was unstoppable now—at least until he killed the others who'd worked on him or wanted to. His eye scanned the room. He saw his clothes in a heap in the corner.

"Stupid," he muttered to himself. His gun was there—or J. W. Carlson's at least. He hobbled back across the room, his legs stiff. The gun in his fist— a real caliber—and the load checked, his spirits, he felt, were lifting. He grabbed his clothes, then went over to the dead body of Genevieve. Unfeelingly, he pushed up her dress and ripped the slip from her waist, then tore it into long strips, these tying around the largest of the wounds on his legs. There wasn't enough material, so he started cannibalizing her dress as well, using the extra material to bandage over the largest of the cuts, some already bleeding through.

He snatched up her straight razor and pocketed

110

it in the trousers laying beside him on the floor, then pulled the pants on, stuffing his shorts and shirt and socks into his pockets for later. He got his feet into his shoes, took anything useful out of his jacket—he couldn't put it on because of the shackles on his wrists—and went to the doorway.

Standing there, the pain now something he could almost live with, Frost heard running sounds from the hallway, but apparently only one man.

"Genevieve!" he heard the German-sounding man say, then in English, "We need you upstairs—Marcel needs a shot and can't give it to himself—we have to calm him—"

The man stopped, walking past Frost as he came through the door. Frost swatted both manacled hands down across the back of the man's neck, then threw himself on the Nazi, the straight razor open in his right hand, slashing it across the man's neck and throat. Frost turned his face away as the arteries spurted blood. It was one of the guys who'd been waiting a turn on him, and as he quickly searched the man's pockets and found a pushbutton knife and the key he sought, Frost rasped, "Better luck next time, sucker."

Working the key, his fingers stiff and aching from the pain in his wrists, was difficult, but in a few seconds he had freed himself. Using the razor, he slashed away the front of the man's blue shirt and used it to bandage his raw and bleeding wrists. Dropping the razor and pushbutton knife in his trouser pocket, Frost grabbed up his jacket and slipped it on. He turned and started toward the door.

He glanced at the Seiko watch with the broken

111

band he found still in his jacket pocket. He realized bitterly that Balsam's kidnappers would be sending back another piece of the Doctor unless the ransom had been paid in the last day — and Frost doubted that. An ear this time, or another finger? The thought revolted him. And, if the Nazis didn't have Balsam — there had been no reason for Liebling to lie — then who did?

As Frost reached the library doors leading into the hallway, he turned and looked toward the stairs leading to the smoky second floor. Marcel was coming down with a submachine gun in his fists.

Chapter Ten

There was nothing Frost could do but fire, the big Patridge front sight on the Gold Cup just falling in line with the notched Elliason rear as he extended his right arm toward the target. The first round caught Marcel in the right arm—Marcel had moved just as Frost had fired—the second round missing. Marcel screamed—not like a man, but like a woman would, Frost thought. As his assailant started running up the steps, his right arm hanging limp at his side, Frost fired again. He brought the muzzle down on the big .45, the 185-grain jacketed hollow point catching Marcel in the rear end, driving the man forward up the steps and onto his face—unmoving, dead.

"Poetic justice!" Frost shouted. Half tempted

113

to go after the submachine gun Marcel had carried, Frost turned on his heel and ran as best he could for the hallway doors leading outside. Liebling and three other men were already starting down the steps, all with subguns in their hands.

The doors were locked, and Frost, his wind up now he felt, took a step back and lashed out with his battered right leg, his foot hammering hard against the central lock of the double wooden doors, the shock telegraphing tremors of pain up through his body.

Frost almost dove through the doorway then, out onto the small cement porch. Submachine gun bursts splintered the doors on both sides of him. Frost heard Leibling shouting, "Get that man!" Frost, on his knees, thrust the pistol in his right hand toward the Nazis coming through the hallway behind him, firing twice, his shots nailing the man to Liebling's right, Liebling himself falling back, his left arm going up to somehow protect his face. Frost fired once more, then again, the slide of the Gold Cup locking open, empty. Dragging himself to his feet, ramming a fresh seven-round magazine up the butt of the Colt and releasing the slide stop, he upped the thumb safety and took off in a lurching run across the courtyard. There were cars at the far side of a long circular driveway and he started toward them.

Halfway across the square courtyard, Frost stopped, whipping off two fast shots toward a half-dozen armed men running toward him from a black Citroen that had just ground to a halt in the driveway. Again, behind him, Frost heard Liebling shouting, "Stop that

114

man – Helmut, you and the others – there he goes! Get the dogs!" As Frost spun on his heel and took off toward the woods on his right, he fired two more shots toward Liebling and the others on the small porch.

His legs aching badly, Frost forced himself to keep picking up his feet, "Pick 'em up and lay em' down," he kept telling himself under his breath. As he reached the edge of the line of trees, he could hear already the yelping of the dogs in the background. Shooting a glance over his shoulder he saw them – a half dozen or more, glistening sleek bodies, muscles rippling as they strained at the leashes holding them back, the redness of their mouths starkly visible against the white of their teeth and the black coats of their bodies.

Dobermans!

The autumn woods were devoid of leaves, except for the evergreen conifers spotted here and there in clumps. As Frost lurched through the entangled branches and vines, his clothes and his flesh ripping against nettles and thorns, the yelping of the Dobermans on his trail grew louder, the pain in his legs more intense.

Stopping for an instant to draw a full breath, he glanced down – his trouser legs were wet and dark with his blood – a perfect trail for the dogs to follow. He started running again, glancing skyward above the treetops to gauge the time at perhaps nine in the morning.

As Frost dragged one foot after the other, his mind raced as well – there was no hope of outrunning the Dobermans or their heavily armed Nazi masters

—his legs were nearly gone from pain and loss of blood and gauging the distance as best he could he guessed he'd run less than a mile. The pistol still held in his hand had a nearly full magazine, plus there was one more loaded spare. The handful of shells loose now in his trouser pocket couldn't amount to more than two or three magazines full. The little Baby Browning .25 with its load would be less than marginal against the men or the dogs. The straight razor would not do against multiple assailants—human or animal. Falling, then pulling himself to his feet, Frost changed direction and headed across a small open clearing about the size of a football field.

He had to get a submachine gun, he determined —his only hope of slightly evening the odds against his pursuers.

Halfway across the clearing, Frost stumbled again. As he pulled himself onto his knees and then started to his feet, he glanced over his shoulder. The Dobermans and their masters were breaking into the field behind him. One of the men dropped down and started firing his submachine gun. Frost, the pistol shaking in his hands from loss of blood, cold and breathing hard, jerked the trigger on the Gold Cup once. The sights wandered into line. The shot—almost miraculously, Frost felt—was good; the subgunner fell back on his haunches, the gun itself shooting wild, one of the dogs nearest the downed man yelping and stumbling, then going down. Frost lobbed another shot—this one going wild as he'd known it would when he touched the trigger—then started running again. As Frost glanced

116

behind him, he could see that three of the remaining five Dobermans had been loosed and were coming at him in a dead run.

Frost reached the boundary of the huge field and turned, his back to a tall thin pine. The nearest Doberman was already going into a lunge, lips curled back, fangs bared. Frost had no choice but to fire, his 185-grain jacketed hollow point hammering into the animal's chest, its effect like a brick wall, the dog falling back. As he turned again to run, he silently cursed the Nazis who'd trained the animals to kill, wishing that the bullet he'd fired in defense of his life could have taken the life of one of the men rather than the animal.

Frost pushed himself hard to up his pace, almost feeling the hot breath of the second and third Dobermans behind him, but daring not to slow his pace and look behind him. Intentionally, he dodged trees and zig-zagged to slow the animals behind him. Starting to jump over a deadfall birch tree, Frost's left foot caught onto a stray branch. He fell – going down hard, forward onto his chest, then rolling as he came out of it, one of the dogs behind him in mid-air and coming down for his throat. Frost threw up his left arm, his feet catching the animal in the midsection, his legs hurling the dog over his head and to the ground. Rolling, another Doberman was coming at him, and again Frost had no choice but to shoot, the two rounds he fired catching the animal in the head – it fell like a punctured balloon.

Hauling himself to his knees, Frost could see the second dog coming at him. He started to fire, but the .45 in his hand was empty, the slide locked back and open. As the animal lunged, Frost thrust the pistol forward, his right fist wrapped around the gunbutt like a street fighter holding a roll of quarters. His right hand struck bone and as his swing cleared, the animal falling away, Frost could see his knuckles coming back covered with blood. Frost's right hand buckled under him as he started to get up, but he tried again, stood, awkwardly changed magazines and sent the slide ramming home, then started running again. Now there were sounds in the trees behind him, the heavy sounds of men running behind dogs and trying to hold the dogs in check at the same time.

As Frost ran, pushing his way through the de-nuded bushes, dodging tree stumps, he shook his right hand to get feeling back into the fingers. Smearing his right hand against his trouser leg, he could see the skin of his knuckles all but sheared away.

Frost had to slow as he reached a dense over-growth of wild hedge, and as he bulled his way through he turned — the men pursuing him would have to slow as well. There would be five of them at least. Dropping to one knee and grasping the pistol in both hands to steady it, he fired as the first man hit the hedge. The single round caught the Nazi at the bridge of his nose between the eyes — there wasn't even a scream as the man heaved backward into his comrades. One of the last two dogs was loose now and lunging over the hedge toward Frost's throat. Frost fired, the .45

slug tearing into the animal. The dog flew off the side to Frost's left. Already, one of the SMGs was opening up. Frost fired toward the sound, his slug hammering into the subgunner's chest, the man collapsing into the hedge, the gun in his dead fingers still firing.

There was a second subgun firing now, and Frost lurched away from it, a burst grazing him in the left shoulder and arm and rolling him to the ground. As the nearest of the Nazis started through the hedge toward him, Frost raised himself on his right elbow and "hip shot" the Gold Cup into the man's groin. The Nazi fell forward, blood pouring through the fingers clasped below his belt over the wound.

Frost, coughing, his breathing labored, his left side burning, fired the .45 again – there were at least two more Nazis and one Doberman. He had no target for the gun – just a target for his hands as he dragged himself across the cold, broken ground. The SMG – a Korean War vintage 9mm Sten. Touching it now with the fingers of his right hand, he let the pistol drop from his fist and grabbed all the way for it.

"Go Fritz!" Frost heard the shout and started bringing up the muzzle of the Sten, but the Doberman was on him, the force of its lunge rolling him across the ground and on top of the dog. His right hand, locked on the SMG, was pinned under the dog. Frost ordered his brain to move the fist there to the animal's throat, the dog's teeth snapping inches from Frost's face. There was a yelp, a stifled bark and the writhing of the animal under him stopped. Frost fell away from it. Two Nazis were coming at him, raising their SMGs to fire. Frost

119

rolled onto his back, the Sten in his right fist, firing — "Eat lead, Goddamn you!" Frost heard himself screaming, at the back of his mind somewhere wondering if he'd gone over the edge, from retaliatory violence to madness.

As both men fell under the fire from the Sten Frost got himself to his knees, falling on the one of the two men who was still moving and smashing the skeletonized buttstock of the automatic weapon against the man's face, Frost realized that perhaps it *was* madness.

Frost lay on the cold ground, his body half covering the body of the dead man beneath him, his breathing painful, the vision in his eye starting to cloud over with colors of gold and red. Weaponless except for the razor and the .25 — and for the moment there he couldn't move — he watched the ground less than a yard away from him. The Doberman he had struck in the throat was lying on his stomach, a low growl coming from its bared lips, the coal black eyes seeming to be staring at Frost's eye.

Coughing and closing his eye with pain, Frost turned his head, then looked again at the dog, forcing his tightly balled fists — rage, cold, pain — to open spreading his palms out to the animal. If the dog lunged, Frost knew, he would be finished — at least until he got his wind.

They lay like that, less than a yard apart. Frost started coughing again, the coughing making him start to lose his breath. The cold in the woods there was racking his body with tremors and he had out run his lungs. Slowly, Frost shuffled through his coat pockets with his right hand, found what felt to be a crumpled package of cigarettes and his lighter. He put the cigarette to his lips and spit it onto the ground. "Damn," he thought, then with his right hand broke away the filter and lit what was left of the menthol cigarette with his Zippo. The first inhalation started him coughing and Frost could no longer control it—Air! his lungs seemed to shout and he saw the gold and red floaters before his eye again, then there was a blur of light and nothing . . .

Frost opened his eye. He could feel that his left cheek was covered with dirt and as he looked at his bloody right hand he could see leaves stuck to the crusted reddish brown across his knuckles. "The dog," he said half aloud, his voice cracking. Shivering, he looked across from him. The Doberman was there, still staring at him, then slinking on its belly started toward him. Frost started to move for the Browning .25 or the razor, but as the dog neared him, he stopped. He stretched out his damaged right hand and the animal licked at it with his tongue, then nuzzled toward him. Standing then, the animal came and stood beside Frost as he lay there on the ground.

Frost pushed himself up on his right elbow, glancing at the drying blood on his left shoulder where the bullets had struck. The dog nuzzled against him again, and Frost in all his experience realized that he couldn't understand why. Looking at the dog, gently, then more roughly stroking its neck, Frost whispered, "Love, not war, huh? Why the hell not?" He got to his knees, then bracing his right hand on the dog—the animal flinched a moment then stood its ground—Frost got himself onto his feet.

Frost stood there a moment, the exertion making him dizzy again, but he didn't pass out. Slowly—he still wasn't a hundred percent certain of the dog—he searched the bodies nearest to him. He found a heavy coat that wasn't too chewed up with gunfire or drenched with blood and pulled it off the dead Nazi who'd worn it, covering his own body with it. He found a fresh Sten gun and three spare magazines. Then he took a sweater from one of the other dead men and packed it against his wounded left shoulder, holding it there with the jacket that he zipped tight across his chest.

Despite the coat, Frost's body still trembled with the cold. Orienting himself—the sun read about noon, he guessed—he started walking, and as he turned he saw the Doberman following behind him, its pace slow and uncertain. Frost remembered what the Nazi had shouted before the dog had lunged. Gambling that it was the animal's name rather than an attack command, Frost turned and looked at the dog, holding out his battered left hand, saying "Fritz!"

The dog stood up, then ran to him, Frost's involuntary reaction to start to raise the muzzle of the Sten gun to defend himself. But the dog stopped and sat on its haunches beside him. Forcing the smile/frown lines on his stubbled face into a grin, Frost bent down and stroked the dog behind the ears. "I usually work solo, fella—but we'll see how it goes."

The Doberman beside him, Frost started out through the trees.

The Seiko that had been in Frost's coat pocket was smashed and his only gauge of time was the declining sun overhead. As he and the dog reached the edge of the tree line, Frost spotted the road less than a hundred yards away. He glanced skyward again.

"Four o'clock, Fritz," he muttered. "Be dark soon. Come on."

In the distance along the ribbon of two lane rough paved road, Frost could see a cross-country bus and he upped his pace, the Doberman bouncing beside him, to intercept the road before the bus passed.

Frost dropped to his knees in the middle of the road, half from exhaustion and half through guile. He realized that it was unlikely the bus would stop for a man that could be seen clearly, clothes covered with blood, a submachine gun in hand, a Doberman at his side. But on his knees, Frost could conceal the gun behind his back, and the bizarre way he knew he looked would be less noticeable at a quick glance that way.

He looked up as the bus sped down the road toward him, his trigger finger tensed in case he would need to fire to stop the bus. Still trembling, his body an unending raw nerve of pain, Frost knew that he could not go on much longer. The rest stops with Fritz beside him had been becoming more and more frequent and of longer duration, and once he had thought he had heard the sound of men in the woods behind him. Liebling? Frost had wondered.

123

The bus was still coming, and as it appeared it would not slow, Frost started to edge the Sten gun from behind his back. But he stopped as the screeching of the brakes on the bus became something he could hear. Frost let his head loll forward, whispering as low as he could, "Easy Fritz – easy boy – shhh."

From the corner of his eye, Frost could see the bus finally stop less than ten yards from where he knelt in the road, see the feet of the driver – he assumed – stepping down and onto the road, slowly, almost hesitantly starting toward him. The feet seemed oddly small.

"Shhh, Fritz," Frost whispered, the dog making a low growl as the feet approached.

The feet stopped, and Frost looked up, sweeping the muzzle of the Sten gun on line as he did. The bus driver, Frost realized, was not a man, but a woman, pudgy looking, like somebody's mother, salt and pepper black and gray hair crammed under a man's uniform hat.

"*Parlez-vous Anglais?*" Frost stumbled.

"*Oui* – a little. From the war."

"I don't . . . Frost started, stopping as an involuntary paroxysm of pain doubled him forward. Then, looking back into her clear blue eyes, he went on, "I don't mean to hurt you or your passengers – Nazis, the neo-Nazis. After me. Get me out of here."

"Nazis?" The woman's voice was hushed, as though the word were evil itself just to speak.

"The ones who've been bombing synagogues, killing children – the neo-Nazis. Did this to me . . . "

124

Frost gestured with his bloodied left hand and pointed with it to his bloodsoaked trousers.

"The Bosche!" She started toward him and Fritz started to growl. "You be quiet," she commanded, while Frost extended his hand to the animal and stroked its neck.

"Come," the woman bus driver said. "Marie Boule has fought the Nazis before."

The woman bent down to him and Frost tried standing, then almost collapsed against her. He watched the woman, her hands now smeared with his blood. "The pigs," she whispered, then shouting at the top of her voice said something Frost could not fathom, but he heard the word "Nazi." There were murmurs of conversation, the word "Nazi" repeated again and again as other arms reached down from the steps of the bus and helped him aboard.

The driver—Marie—pushed aside a basket of flowers and helped Frost stretch back on the long seat behind the driver's seat. "What are they saying?" Frost asked.

"That if the Nazis—if they come for you, they will get more than they bargained for. Your dog— he will not come. Hurry!"

"Fritz," Frost shouted, and as he craned his neck toward the doorway, he could see the animal leaping aboard.

There was a pneumatic hiss from the doors as Marie slid behind the wheel, her generous stomach, Frost could just make out, pressed hard against the wheel so that it must have rubbed each time she moved it. Frost could hear the gears grinding, the brakes screeching, and a loud thud as she apparently remembered the emergency brake. And then, as Frost closed his eye, he could feel the bus starting to move and the warm breath of the dog Fritz beside his face.

Frost opened his eye and it was dark except for a few small ceiling lights in the bus. There was a man kneeling beside him, wrapping a makeshift bandage on his left hand. Frost looked at him, sharply, confused.

"It is all right," the man whispered.

Then Frost noticed the clerical collar. "We are a half hour away from town—I am a priest. I have had some medical training."

"Mercy, isn't it," Frost asked, his voice cracking and his throat dry.

"Do you mean 'mercy' or thank you?" the cleric asked, his voice low but sounding almost amused.

"Both," Frost said, then added, "I guess."

"Hey—you are awake no?"

It was the voice of Marie, the driver, and Frost craned his neck to answer.

"He is awake," the priest said.

"None of the Nazi pigs yet, *mon ami*." Then, her voice softening, she said, "I knew an American once, during the war—he was with your OSS. Do you still have that?"

"We have," Frost started, coughed, then went on, "the CIA and the Special Forces—between the two they accomplish the same thing."

"He was a nice boy," she said and then cleared her throat and fell silent.

"Do you wish a cigarette?" the priest asked Frost.

"I found these in the pocket of the jacket I removed from you."

Frost started to say no, but then noticed they weren't the menthol ones—Players, instead. "Yes, please," he said, the priest then taking the lighter—Frost recognized it as his own—and putting it to the cigarette, inhaling and putting the cigarette between Frost's lips.

"American!" It was Marie's voice again.

"What is it?" Frost asked.

"There are two cars blocking the road ahead—I cannot go around them and if I ram through them, I do not know."

"I can," Frost started to say, trying to get up.

"We can, American," the woman said, her voice taking on a strange sound Frost recognized but at the back of his mind had somehow thought was missing from the world.

"Help me," Frost said, the priest bending down over him and helping him into a sitting position. "Help me with my legs," Frost said, then with the priest aiding him, he swung his feet to the floor.

"Here, Father—hand this to our American." From the corner of his eye Frost saw the outline of his pistol in Marie's hand held up over her head.

"The submachine gun," Frost stammered.

"I was not always a priest—God forgive me," the cleric said.

Frost could feel the bus beneath him slowing as he mechanically checked the Gold Cup for a loaded magazine and a chambered round, half remembering recharging the pistol and the empty magazines shortly after setting out back in the woods with

Fritz. Fritz, beside Frost, was starting the low growl again.

Pulling himself to the edge of the seat, Frost strained his eye to look past Marie's massive shoulder and to the road ahead. The headlights of the cars were glaring toward the bus. "They'll be armed," Frost said, his face a foot away from Marie's ear.

"And so are we," she answered matter-of-factly. "My father, my brother, my older sister—they were killed in the Resistance fighting those—" and she noticeably cut herself off, her voice cracking.

"I'm sorry," Frost said, somehow wishing that he knew the words in French and that that would somehow deepen their sincerity.

Frost felt the priest's hand touch his shoulder a moment.

"Quiet, Fritz—shhh," he rasped as the dog growled beside him.

The bus came to a complete stop, and Frost, beyond the glare of the headlight in the otherwise pitch blackness of the road, could see four figures silhouetted, moving slowly toward the bus.

Frost heard a shout, the words in French which he could not understand.

"Where is the safety catch on this gun?" Frost heard the priest muttering.

Reaching across his gun hand with his bandaged left hand, Frost felt in the darkness and fumbled the catch clear on the gun the priest held.

Startled at hearing English from the men outside the bus, Frost turned toward the doors. "American—come out or all aboard the bus will die—you are aboard—this we know."

128

"I will open the doors – then shoot," Marie whispered, her words barely audible.

There was the pneumatic hiss, and as the doors startled slowly to part, Frost heard someone shouting in guttural German. Then the door began to shatter with submachine gun fire. Frost and the priest beside him opened fire simultaneously, Frost dropping forward onto his knees on the floor.

Already, Frost could hear Marie grinding the gears of the long throw transmission, hot brass from his own pistol and the priest's submachine gun flying in his face in the confined space, screams from the other passengers, catcalls and hoots from some of the others all blending into a cacophony of anger – Frost could feel it as though it were somehow telepathic.

Shuffling forward on his knees, Fritz barking maddeningly beside him, Frost was slapping a fresh magazine up the butt of the Gold Cup as the bus started lurching forward. A Nazi with a pistol in his hand was clinging to the doorframe, and Frost raised his pistol and thrust it forward as he thumbed the slidestop down, then jerked the Colt's trigger. The muzzle of his gun was less than a foot away from the Nazi's face. As the bullet impacted the man's head exploded like a grenade and the body flew back, one foot caught inside the doorway as the bus picked up speed; then all that was left was a shoe, the shattered doors closed around it.

The bus smashed forward into the two cars – both Citroens Frost thought – and slowed, the sound of metal grating against metal, of the straining bus – all this and the incessant gunfire on all sides, screams from inside the bus. Then with a sudden jerk the bus was moving again and the gunfire was all behind them now.

Frost reached down to pet the Doberman, but as he did he felt the priest's hand. Frost looked down and in the semi-darkness he could see the dog's sleek black body lying still beside him, the neck bent down at an angle against the side of Frost's shoe.

Frost moved his hand roughly past the priest to the dog's head, touched it between the ears, then took his hand away, wet—the feeling of blood something that was somehow unmistakable to Frost.

"Aww—Fritz . . ." Frost groaned, touching his hand one more time to the dog's head, then seeing the priest beside him—the dog dead between them—unfolding a newspaper and placing it over the animal's head.

"American!"

It was Marie's voice, and Frost turned back to the woman. "What is it?"

"One of their bullets—the engine is starting to ohh, the English. What is it?"

"What," Frost said, "lost compression?"

"*Oui*," she said, her voice suddenly sounding tired. "That is what."

"Are there police in the town?" Frost said.

"Very few—and they might not all be on duty. If there is a gunbattle in the town, there are people there who will be killed."

Frost looked behind them, three headlights coming up fast from behind. "Creamed one of their headlights," he muttered half to himself.

Dragging himself to his feet and edging forward beside her, Frost said, "Can you use the size of this thing against those cars?" Looking back he saw one coming up beside them.

"*Oui*," she said. "Yes, of course." Her voice was alive sounding again and Frost found himself touching his battered left hand to her shoulder a moment. "There is a curve just ahead before we enter the town—and a drop down the hillside. Yes . . . "

"Here," Frost said, turning to the priest, "give me that. Frost took the Sten gun, turning the butt toward the window on the long seat just behind Marie, then rapping it hard against the glass, the ordinance steel framework shattering the glass outward. Then he used the skeletonized buttstock again to knock away the remaining shards of glass. He forced first the gun, then his right arm and shoulder, then his head, through the window, the wind from the bus's slipstream buffetting him from behind as he looked back down the road toward the two Citroens pursuing them.

The car with just a single headlight was flanking the rear of the bus now. As Frost turned the muzzle of the Sten toward it, he could see the outline of a man leaning out the passenger side window, then the flashes of light as the submachine gun in his hands started chattering toward the bus's tires. Marie—fear, Frost thought, but instantly dismissed the idea—jerked the bus and Frost lost his balance a moment; then getting the Sten gun in his right hand on line again, Frost opened fire.

His trigger finger working like a piston, making perfect three shot bursts, Frost poured his fire toward the Citroen's center of mass—the windshield.

131

The car fell away, slowing, dropping behind them, the subgunner pulling himself back inside the window. Frost held his fire. Even in the darkness, by the light of the pursuing cars' headlamps, he could see a rock face rising to the inside of the road.

"Marie!" Frost could hear the priest shouting in his ear, "This is where the hillside is—she tells you to hold on!"

Frost glanced to his left, clapped his injured left hand to the priest's arm, then turned his attention back behind them—the Citroen with the single headlight was coming up fast in the opposite lane.

Frost's right fist balling around the weapon he held, in his mind he was shouting to Marie—"Do it now!" The subgunner in the lead Citroen was leaning out his window again, firing, and Frost thought he saw a puff of dust or smoke—he couldn't tell which—coming from the rear of the bus. Then, even above the noise of the slipstream wind against his ears, he could hear screams from the passengers in the back of the bus.

Frost could see the reason why: flames, blowing hot in the rush of air the bus was making in its headlong lunge down the road, the lights showing the face of the Nazi subgunner leaning out the window of the Citroen. As the flames flashed brighter, Frost could see the man clearly for an instant—white teeth showing from lips curled back in a snarl against the rush of wind. He shoved his Sten gun inside the bus, snatching the Gold Cup from his trouser band, and pointing it at arms' length back out the window alongside the bus. The subgunner was starting to fire again, sparks flashing from the steel shell of the bus as the subgun poured its bullets toward the fire near the fuel system.

As Frost squinted over the rear sight, he almost thought he could see the Nazi turning his head, glaring back at him—a recognition somehow on the subgunner's face. Frost squeezed the trigger on the Gold Cup once. The head of the subgunner snapped back, the SMG flying from his hands, the car falling away, the man's body swinging limp and dead from the car window.

Marie, Frost could feel it as he almost lost his balance—was starting to use the bus's bulk. Tucking his head back inside, he glanced across the bus and through the shoot-out windows opposite him; he could see the second Citroen coming up behind them, then vanishing in a blind spot the side of the bus itself made. Then Frost heard it—the sound of metal grating against metal again, the bus shaking, the screech of tires or brakes. As the bus pulled ahead, Frost lurched toward the rear of the bus. And over the flames there, Frost could see the headlights of the second Citroen turning skyward, a flash of light . . . And then there was nothing but a ball of flame rolling down the darkened hillside behind them, its light illuminating the sky as apparently the Citroen's gas tank ruptured—and a fireball reached upward, then vanished.

"Everybody to the front of the bus," Frost shouted. The faces of the people, glowing red in the reflected light of the flames, looking uncomprehending, and Frost shouted over his shoulder, "Father—help me!" The priest was beside him in an instant, Frost, leaning against the seat railings to keep from collapsing, was pushing people toward the front of the bus.

He could barely hear the rattle of subgun fire. Straining to see beyond the flames, Frost could make out the second Citroen, the one with a single headlight, coming up fast behind them.

Turning and looking forward, Frost could see in the light from the bus's headlamps that they were entering the town. "The brakes!" he could hear Marie shouting over the din. And then Frost started pushing his way forward, past the women, the few children, past the armsful of packages and baskets, past the screams in his ears, and the hands tugging at his arms.

"For God's sake, out of my way!" Frost heard himself shouting. Already, from halfway along the length of the bus, Frost could see a massive stone wall looming up in front of them, and over the sound of the screams of the passengers, the slipstream along the windowless bus, he could hear Marie. He didn't know the words—French?, he wondered absently as he struggled forward, or just desperation making her words unintelligible.

As Frost passed the last of the passengers, he could see Marie clearly now, the wheel locked under the prominent knuckles of her incongruously tiny fists, the wall less than a dozen yards ahead.

"Miles to kilometers—how is that . . . " Frost was muttering to himself as he glanced toward the speedometer, throwing himself in front of Marie. His right fist locked onto the wheel and he pushed, the force of her hands, their deathgrip on the wheel,

134

even the resistance of the wheel against her body making it even harder for him. He heard himself shouting something as he threw his weight against the wheel and the bus lurched to the left. The screams grew louder, there was a maddening screech of rubber and Frost threw his right hand up over his head as he fell across Marie, the bus skidding broadside into the massive stone wall.

Angrily, Frost looked up, his head sore. He glared at the window support—he'd struck his head there, he thought. Shaking his head to clear it, he could hear the screams of the passengers now, louder than before.

He pushed himself up from Marie—"Come on—let's get everyone out of here!"

The back of the bus was a roaring fireball. Already women were pushing children through the shot-out windows, the door sealed against the wall into which they'd crashed.

Looking around, Frost saw the priest, the thin man—it was the first time Frost had really noticed him—helping a woman to clamber out through a window. Frost started grabbing people and shoving them through the windows. One man already afire, Frost snatched up a coat from the floor and beat at the flames as he pushed the man to safety.

"Get out, Father!" Frost screamed. Frost saw no one else aboard. The priest jumped through and as Frost started, he looked forward. It was Marie, standing beside one of the forward seats, paralyzed with fear. In a flash of recognition, he understood. She was fat, her massive bulk would not allow her through the window. A small explosion from the back of the bus threw Frost forward onto his knees. He looked up, felt at his belt. The .45 was still there and it was in his hand almost like something alive that had sprung into his fingers because he'd wished it so. Levelling the gun toward Marie, he saw her staring at him, her eyes level, sparkling in the reflected light of the inferno behind him, her head nodding in resignation. Frost fired, his first round hammering into the forward windshield, the left panel shattering. He fired twice more, all but clearing the major shards from the frame. Stumbling forward, Frost pushed Marie toward the window, then with the slide of the Gold Cup, hacked savagely at the remaining glass in the windshield, then started pushing her toward it. "Come on — jump!"

She was through. Glancing behind him, Frost dove headlong through the window and landed half on his feet. Hauling himself up and grabbing at Marie's elbow he pushed forward, falling to the ground and dragging the woman down with him as the bus behind them exploded.

Exhaling hard, Frost looked up. The bus was nothing now but a long low line of flames. As he started to his feet, he saw the priest coming to help him. They both helped the portly Marie. She took Frost's hand. She was fat, past middle age. But her eyes sparkled and as she held his right hand in both of hers, Frost leaned down and kissed the left cheek that glowed in the heat from the flames.

Chapter Eleven

They had hidden Frost when the police came, and it was more than a day before he could even uncomfortably move from the bed they'd forced him into. Stiff now, his legs and left arm and shoulder swathed in bandages beneath the borrowed clothes he wore, the Gold Cup stuffed in his trouser band, Frost walked as inconspicuously as he could toward the tiny gray Fiat. The priest had told him he should steal it—it wouldn't be reported for a day, time enough to get to Paris.

Frost had asked to whom the car belonged, and the priest had answered, "Someone who hated the Nazis more than you could—but never mind." Then the cleric had changed the subject. Frost knew he shouldn't but he turned and shot a wave behind him—the pudgy Marie Boule and rapier-thin Father Renard were standing in the doorway of the church, waving back.

The second Citroen, the one with the single headlamp, had not followed the flaming bus into the village two nights before and Frost didn't deceive himself that he was through with the Nazis. And, as he checked the calendar window on the watch borrowed from the priest, he saw that today again there would be another grisly message from Doctor Balsam's kidnappers. What would it be this time? Perhaps the man was dead already?

The drive to Paris was tiring to Frost, still weak from loss of blood and the exertion he had endured. After he ditched the Fiat in what he hoped would be a conspicuous place for it to be found by the Paris police, he walked two blocks and took a taxi into the suburbs to the Mossad headquarters. There was no time, he reasoned, to attempt to contact Sheila Balsam and go through channels.

He dismissed the taxi two blocks from the house and walked the rest of the way, but when he arrived at the house he found it deserted. Walking up the street and down to make certain that he had the right house—Frost tried convincing himself that somehow in the difference between darkness and daylight he could have made an error—he only comfirmed to himself that Mossad headquarters was no longer.

A residential neighborhood, there were no taxis in view so, weary now to the point of collapse, he forced himself to walk toward the Metro station, snapping up the collar of his quilted jacket against the cold, his hands crammed into his pockets. He hadn't thought to borrow gloves.

He took the Metro to what he guessed would be the first really busy metropolitan area, then left the train, found a taxicab a block away from the station and took it to Sheila Balsam's hotel.

He'd half hoped that he'd find her waiting in the lobby, but wasn't disappointed when he found her absent. And, after checking with the desk clerk and struggling over the language hurdle until the man called another hotel employee who spoke English, Frost wasn't really surprised that they had never heard of Sheila Balsam. Nor could they recall a young woman matching her description having stayed there recently.

As Frost was about to leave, the English speaking clerk said, "You would not be a Monsieur Frosty, Monsieur?"

"Frost," he corrected.

"*Oui* — Frost."

"Frost — why," he asked.

"A gentleman — he did not leave his name — left a small package for you."

"Let me see it," Frost said. It was a brown manila envelope, padded, the type used for mailing small and breakable packages. Inside was five thousand dollars in cash and his watch and two packs of Camels — all he'd left behind except for his clothes. There was a note, the message two words: "Sorry — Captain." Frost assumed the broad characters of the note were in Karkov's hand. Frost dropped the envelope inside his jacket, nodded to the clerk and walked out of the lobby. Slipping his watch on—he'd left the borrowed one in the Fiat's glove box—he hailed a taxi, but then waved the driver on, the driver muttering something Frost couldn't understand about Americans.

His natural impulse had been to head back to his hotel, But Frost now thought better of that. The Sûreté would certainly be looking for a one-eyed man and know it was him. There had to be some witnesses to the bus ride who let the notice of his eyepatch slip, and that would certainly signal Fouchard that it was Frost. And the Nazis—somehow Frost was certain that Liebling had not been killed in the auto Marie had forced off the road with her bus—would be searching for him as well.

Frost started walking, hunching his shoulders against the cold of the Paris streets, realizing that here too he wasn't safe. He could be spotted by the police at any time. He stopped in front of a large men's store and pretended to study the contents of the window display. He had to get out of France—there was nothing at present, he realized, he could do for Balsam. His passport—in the hotel safe—would only serve to get him arrested at the airport anyway.

Mentally determining to contact Bess in London and somehow get her to help, Frost started to walk on, shoving his cold hands in his pockets and this time feeling the five thousand dollars he had transferred there. Turning, he entered the store, purchasing a pair of Levis—ridiculously expensive in Europe he thought—a Western shirt, a wide belt and a pair of track shoes. He found a warm looking fisherman's knit sweater, heavy sweat socks, underwear and a brown leather jacket. Telling the salesman he wanted to try on the Levis, he changed completely in the wardrobe room, walking out and handing over cash for his purchases. On the way out, he stopped again and purchased a pair of dark-lensed polarized sunglasses, his old borrowed clothes in an expensive looking box under his arm.

At the first alley he passed, he dropped the box beside a trash can, stripped off his eyepatch and put on the dark glasses. Pocketting the patch, he pulled on the gloves he'd purchased and started walking again.

After ten minutes, Frost found a "warm" looking restaurant, large enough where he'd be able to find someone speaking English. When the waiter and Frost discovered they could not communicate, the man held up a hand, gesturing for Frost to wait. In a moment another waiter appeared, this man speaking excellent English. Frost—despite the hour—purchased steak and eggs and hash-browned potatoes—the latter involving quite a test, Frost thought, of his powers of description. By the time he had finished his third cup of coffee, the food arrived. Frost devoured it ravenously, ordering a double of Seagrams Seven and what sounded—by the waiter's description—to be something like an apple turnover. It was, and Frost ordered another drink, going to a public phone in the back of the restaurant while the waiter brought the whiskey.

It took less time than Frost had expected for his long distance collect call to get through to London. The voice on the other end did not belong to Bess, told the operator to wait. In a moment though, Frost heard the familiar alto he loved on the line, saying, "Yes operator, this is Miss Stallman—I'll accept the charges. Frost? Is that you?"

"Yeah, kid," he groaned, his face breaking into a grin.

"Ohh, Frost—thank God. I thought you were dead. The Police—well, you know."

"Yeah—the bus right?" Frost said, lowering his voice, hoping the barman nearby didn't understand English.

"Right—can you get to me? I have something you need, desperately."

"Good—and somethin' else I need, too," Frost said.

"There are laws against talking that way on the telephone, Mister."

"Shut up," he said, then, "can you—if you understand my problems here—recommend someone to help expedite the situation. Hmmm?"

"What?" she said. "Somebody listening to you Frost?"

"Could be," he said, noncommittally, turning deeper into the wall kiosk.

"Yeah—Al Best, with my Bureau—you remember the name?"

"Gotcha—gonna fly now—see you soon."

"Hey, Frost," the voice at the other end of the line spoke in his ear.

"Yeah—I know—I gotta stop callin' collect, right?"

"Yeah—that and I love you. Be careful."

142

"Always said you were silly—but I love you, too. Soon," and Frost hung up the receiver. He scanned the Paris metro phone book and found the address of Bess's Bureau's office there, but decided against calling. He'd gamble, he felt, that Al Best was in. Likely too—he knew Bess well—she would be calling the guy from London to tell him to expect a visitor.

When Frost went back to his table, his drink was waiting. He sat there for another ten minutes, smoking and staring out the window into the street. He paid with American cash again, then walked back out onto the street. He found a taxi two blocks away and gave the driver an address that turned out to be less than three blocks from Sûreté head-quarters. Frost had an anxious moment as the driver passed the building.

The news bureau offices were on the second floor and Frost—still shy of elevators—found a stairwell and walked. He was feeling better after the meal, but the stairs still brought back the pain in his legs. He knocked on the frosted glass office door, tried the knob—it was locked—and knocked again.

"She said you had a mustache—not that dirt stain over your lip."

Frost turned to his left, automatically reaching under his coat.

"Yeah, you must be Frost—I'm Al Best."

Frost stared down the hallway to the wooden door half opened and a pot bellied, balding man in his late fifties standing one foot into the wall. "You were almost the late Al Best." Frost walked the two steps down to the man and extended his right hand.

Best's handshake felt warm to Frost, dry and firm — a solid handshake in any man's reckoning.

"Bess is a good woman — and a damned good reporter. What's she see in you?" Best said as he walked into his office, Frost following. "Close the door," he added.

"I'm charming like you are," Frost said. "She give you an idea what I need?"

"Yeah," Best said, easing himself into a leather chair and silhouetting himself against the half-curtained window behind his desk, sunlight streaming through it.

"Can you do it?" Frost asked.

"Why should I?"

"Like you said," Frost answered, "Bess is a good woman."

"Yeah, but good doesn't always mean bright. I'm trying to decide if I had a daughter — which I don't — would I let her hang around with a guy like you. Maybe Bess'd be better off sitting around pining for you while you were in the pokey."

Unbidden, Frost sat down in the chair in front of the desk, turning it to avoid looking into the sunlight.

"She said you wore an eyepatch and a mustache — what? You think you're in some damned pirate movie or somethin'?"

"So?"

"Well? You got no mustache — just some stubble — and no eyepatch."

Frost took off his glasses, turning his face so the scar where his eye should have been was easily seen. "The eye's permanently gone — the mustache is just temporary—but it's comin' back. I wish I could say the same thing about the eye." Frost put the glasses back on.

"How'd you lose the eye—pickin' your nose and your finger slipped or somethin'?"

"No," Frost groaned, "I used that one already. Actually," he smiled, "It's not much of a story really."

"Go ahead," Best said. "Illuminate me, Captain Frost."

"Well, this one year when I was in college, I got a job working in a candy factory as a chocolate dipper," Frost began. "Grueling work—sticky business, no pun intended, of course. Well, things were going along well until that one fateful day in July, I recall, when the representative from Electro Dip Automatic Candy Making Machine and Comptometer arrived. It was the first day we were to use the new Electronic Pneumatic Depitting Machines on the chocolate covered cherry line. Hand-operated, the machines would supposedly pluck the pit and dump the cherry into the chocolate vats at the same time in one beautifully fluid motion. And," Frost said, "let me tell you, they were something to see. Professor Feldspar Cornbun—the designer—even came to the factory himself to supervise implementation of the Electronic Pneumatic Depitting Machines.

"Well, being a college kid and all, they sort of figured I'd be fascinated with the magical new labor saving device so they put me on the line with one of the machines right beside the boss's nephew, Bonhomme McChurl. Well, Bonhomme wasn't the most co-ordinated fella you'd want to meet—kept twirling the Electronic Pneumatic Depitter by this trigger guard-like thing that housed the one button that you mashed down when you wanted to do the Electronic Pneumatic Depitting.

"Well, things were going along okay for the—oh, how many were there?—yes, the years do dull the memory—the first three and one-quarter dozen maraschino cherries. I guess Bonhomme was getting a little cocky or something—I don't know. Well, my safety glasses fell off because the bridge of my nose got greasy when one of the cherries squirted me. I always heeded those signs that read, 'Wear your safety glasses unless you want to lose an eye.' Well, I just bent over double quick to get my glasses and that's when Bonhomme McChurl started going into his twirling number with the Electronic Pneumatic Depitter Device.

"It was malfunctioning," Frost went on, "and that was clear to see. Instead of popping the pits, it was just grabbing the whole cherry and tossing it into the chocolate vat, then up onto the drying conveyor. As I bent down, the depitter that Bonhomme was twirling just went and electronically pneumatically depitted my left eye right out of my head."

Shaking his head, Frost said, "Oh, the pain was excruciating. But I was still able to see out of my unpitted eye and I watched my left eye tumble down—spit so to speak by the Electronic Pneumatic Handheld Depitter—right into the chocolate vat and onto the conveyor belt."

"What a horrible story!" Best said, smiling.

"Yeah, but that's not the worst of it," Frost

146

added. "This woman bought a box of depitted mara-schino cherry candy a month later and sued the company. One of the ladies in her bridge club swallowed my eye."

"I can't see where Bess admires you for your sense of humor," Al Best said.

Frost looked at the man and stopped smiling. "You gonna help me or what?" he asked.

"I'm gonna help you for Bess's sake. You're a mercenary, I understand, and I don't like mercenaries. I covered the Congo back then and I never met a merc who endeared himself to my heart."

Smiling, "Well," Frost said, "just never met me then, did you?"

"You realize I can get myself deported or worse for getting you a phony passport? And what about the damned eye. You can't hide that very well, can you now?"

"It's been done before," Frost said. "Passport photo gets retouched to put in the other eye and I show up wearing a bandage or dark glasses—no sweat."

"You escape out of countries a lot, hmmm?"

"Well," Frost said, "now that you mention it . . . "

Chapter Twelve

Bess, her blond hair parted in the middle and shoulder length by now—the first time Frost had met her he'd cut her hair with a fighting knife to save her life*—had an office and everything, he thought, impressed. He'd caught her by surprise and she was halfway across her office and to the door to get to him when Frost pushed past the pretty receptionist and walked inside. Bess came into his arms, his right hand grabbing her at the waist, his left hand settling comfortably on her rear end as he kissed her, her lips moist and tasting just as he remembered them.

"Let me look at you," he said, pushing her back to arm's length. She turned around for him, half-

* Mercenary # 1 —The Killer Genesis

148

giggling as she did. She wore a plain navy blue dress, some thin gold chains around her neck and small gold earrings.

He started to pull her into his arms again as he looked beyond her paper littered desk, then turned toward the man sitting on the small sofa by the far wall. "What the hell is Fouchard doing here, kid?" Frost said, his hand going to his pocket to fish out a Camel, Fouchard's hand slipping toward his coat as well, but coming back empty.

"Well—"

"Well?" Frost looked at her. Her eyes were green, searching his and—Frost felt—trying to tell him in her motherly way that everything was all right. Without an answer, Frost coiled his left arm around her waist and touched his lips to her forehead, whispering, "You're the one person I trust—it's okay."

Then raising his voice and turning to Fouchard, Frost said, "Well, Inspector?"

"He—aah, he came to me," Bess said.

"You are a hard man to keep under surveillance, *mon ami*—we lost you completely after the affair with the bus—my counter-terrorist squad, that is. Here, you will no doubt need these," Fouchard reached into his briefcase and produced Frost's silvery looking Metalifed Browning High Power 9mm, the spare magazines, his Gerber MkI boot knife. Setting them on the corner of Bess's desk, he reached into the inside breast pocket of his suit and produced an American passport. He tossed it across the few feet separating them, and Frost caught it. Frost glanced inside—it was stamped for a legal exit from France.

149

"Why did you do this?" Frost asked.

"I need your help, Hank—your luggage from the hotel, your shoulder holster, everything else is at the apartment of Mademoiselle Stallman."

"You need my help for what?" Frost snapped, ignoring the rest of what the Sûreté Inspector had said.

"It is a detailed account—a long story, as you Americans say. Why don't we all sit down?" Fouchard said, crossing his legs and leaning back on the sofa.

Frost, nodding his head deferentially, sat in a leather armchair across from Fouchard, a small, low coffee table strewn with magazines separating them. Bess, reaching down to her intercom, said, "Helene—could you get us some coffee?" Then she sat on the arm of Frost's chair, letting her hand trail across his shoulders.

Lighting a Camel in the blue yellow flame of his Zippo, Frost said to Fouchard, "Okay?"

"As I indicated," the inspector began, "we have been following you—do you have any idea how many French laws you have broken, *mon ami?*"

"A lot, I bet," Frost said. "Depends on when you started following me."

"From the moment you left my offices until you escaped from the Nazis in the country house—the affair with the woman you know as Miss Balsam" Frost felt Bess's fingers digging into his neck—"your captivity by the Mossad, then your eventual capture by the Nazis. The brawl, I think you call it, in the bar when you were trying to find a gun,—everything."

150

"Why didn't you guys step in?" Frost asked.

"What—when the Nazis were torturing you? I confess that we had lost your trail, arriving after you had already apparently freed yourself. We would have interfered had we been there."

"I bet," Frost groaned, stubbing out his cigarette in a small marble ashtray.

The young woman Frost had seen in Bess's outer office came in with a large tray, set it on the end of the coffee table and poured three large white cups of coffee, setting them on the table approximately in front of Frost, Bess and Fouchard. "I got some pastries, too," the girl said, taking a plate and setting it on the side of the table.

"Thanks, Helene," Bess said, smiling as the girl left.

Turning back to Fouchard, Frost asked, "Why didn't you guys step in when you had a fistful of Nazis back there at the house?"

"We were hoping they would lead you to Dr. Balsam—very simple. So now, I must ask, are you any closer to finding the good Professor?"

"No—farther away as a matter of fact," Frost said, his voice sounding tired. "They don't have Balsam, don't seem to know who does—thought I could tell them. And if *they* don't, I have no idea who does."

"The men who attacked you at the airport in Chicago—their police records indicate that they were American Nazis. The men who attacked you at the hotel in Paris—they too, our sources confirm, were Nazis. But we know nothing certain about the identity of the men who attacked you and our of-

151

ficers on the roadside and kidnapped the Doctor. Perhaps they were not Nazis."

"What?" Frost said. "Why all the Jew stuff?" then turning to Bess, he said in a low voice, "Sorry kid." Looking back at Fouchard, "Why the Swastika, why the brutality of leaving Balsam's finger? I mean, it was obvious *they* had him."

"This," Fouchard began, pausing a moment, "we do not know. It seems apparent that the Professor is in danger of losing his life. The parts of— forgive me," and he made a small nod toward Bess, "the parts returned are from Balsam. And there lies perhaps the most interesting thing—it is how I first decided that your Mademoiselle Stallmann needed to be involved. Mademoiselle and I arrived at identical conclusions through differing lines of research."

"And what is it," Frost said, glancing to Bess still sitting on the chair arm beside him.

"Frost," she said, her voice almost a whisper, "Dr. Balsam is dying—terminally ill with cancer. There's evidence it has metasticized—the initial tumor has broken up and entered his bloodstream. He could die within days or weeks or months. A year would be overly optimistic."

"Ohh shit," Frost said, turning his face away and starting to light a cigarette, then sliding it back in the package, thinking better of it for the moment.

"Mademoiselle Stallman," Fouchard said, "discovered this through some unorthodox prying into Dr. Balsam's medical records. We discovered it through a chance further analysis of the finger sent to us—the blood. The two additional fingers we have received as

152

further warnings since the kidnapping—the latest yesterday—bear out the findings."

Frost exhaled a long sigh, decided to light a cigarette anyway and slumped down in the chair. No one spoke for a moment. Frost looked at the plate of sweet rolls, said, "What the hell?" and took one—pineapple.

Frost sipped at the coffee—it was too strong and bitter tasting but he drank it anyway. "Evidently whoever kidnapped him doesn't know he's dying," he remarked absently.

"There is another possibility," Fouchard said, his voice emotionless.

"What?" Frost asked, turning and looking into Fouchard's eyes.

"That perhaps the good Professor is in complicity with his kidnappers—that there is some purpose which has not yet come to light as to why the Professor himself wishes to have ten million dollars in diamonds at his disposal. With his prognosis, it would not be hard to imagine him allowing the severance of the digits we have received. They are from his left hand—he is right-handed."

"Isn't that about as clever as saying I let my left eye be plucked out because the right eye was stronger to begin with?" Frost said mockingly.

"I have reason to understand, from the tone in which your Mademoiselle Stallmann speaks of you, and the tone of your meeting here before my eyes that you are both—ehh."

"Lovers?" Frost raised his right eyebrow and smiled at Fouchard. "We are."

"Would you not have given your eye for her life if necessary—you are the sort of man I think who would?"

153

Frost considered Fouchard's remark a moment, looked at Bess then with his only good eye, then squeezed her hand. Turning to Fouchard, he said in a low voice, "You think that Balsam has some reason worth giving up everything for – something as important as a love?"

"Or a hate – "

Conversation died while Frost, Bess and Fouchard finished their coffee. When it resumed he learned that Balsam had no daughter – Sheila Balsam was really a Mossad agent named Marita Litski. The Sûreté had started keeping tabs on Bess immediately after her cable to Frost in Paris – assuming that if they were to lose track of Frost he would contact her – which is what he had immediately done, he realized.

"Why are you letting the Mossad operate like this?" Frost asked.

"They are the Secret Service of a more or less friendly nation. Besides, I am using them – without their knowledge – to track down the French Nazi movement. You must understand that I am somewhat limited in manpower. I can trust my counter-terrorist squad implicitly. But other portions of the French police services may have been infiltrated to a degree, however minor, by the very Nazis we seek. If I were to utilize the manpower of the police establishment, I could locate the Nazi leadership, but they would no longer be visible – since someone would have passed them word. If I use an all out search, the Nazis will simply go to ground – a worse situation than we presently have. So, I use the Mossad. I know they have an agent somewhere in our services, but that does not bother me at present."

"I'll go back to my original question," Frost said, lighting a cigarette. "What is it that you want me to do?"

"Quite simple, really," Fouchard said, a smile crossing his lips. "Far less difficult than when you rescued that young lady — Felicity was it? — from the turtlemen."

Frost laughed, Bess looking perplexed. "Hey, wait a minute — what turtlemen?"

"He asked me about my eye," Frost started, "and you know," and he waved his hand.

"Turtlemen!" Bess said, her tone one of mocking disgust.

"What then?" Frost asked Fouchard.

"The society before which Professor Balsam was to speak," Fouchard began. "They have collected the ten million dollars in diamonds. They have arranged with the kidnappers to forego sending back another — another one of their grisly calling cards tomorrow morning. The ransom will be paid on the following morning. If I divert one of my officers, there is substantial chance that it will be noticed by the Nazis, or the terrorists, whoever they are, who are holding Balsam. I want you to be in the wooded area designated for the ransom drop, then to follow whoever picks up the ransom. You have — what is the French expression you Americans have borrowed — yes, carte blanche. You have carte blanche in the matter. Do whatever is necessary to find their hideout. Then, my counter-terrorist squad will step in."

"What if Balsam gets croaked?" Frost asked.

"Killed? We are experienced in handling such matters. There should be little risk of this. You are a professional soldier, a jungle fighter. Tracking a terrorist through a swampy wooded area should not be so difficult. We have made certain arrangements for appropriate vehicles to be spotted around the area should you need transportation. You will have a radio – you can call us in at any time."

"What if they get out by air?" Frost asked.

"We can call in helicopters to follow. And, if we lose the man or woman, at least there may be some chance, however slight, that Balsam will be released without further harm. The actual ten million dollars worth of diamonds will be paid. The colleagues of Doctor Balsam who raised the ransom were adamant about this. Yet they were sufficiently realistic to realize that such an attempt to follow the kidnappers was necessary."

"All right," Frost said. "All right, I'll take a stab at it."

"Good – then you can leave for Paris tomorrow afternoon." Gesturing with his right hand, Fouchard smiled at Frost, then at Bess, saying, "You are free until then."

Chapter Thirteen

"You are going to get killed if you keep up this crap, Frost. Then what the hell am I going to do. Be a widow before I'm a bride? Well, dammit, answer me!"

Frost looked at Bess across the dinner table, smiled and said, "Picky, picky."

"Picky, picky!" she almost screamed. "Ohhh!"

"Now wait, huh," Frost said, extending his hand to her over their coffee cups.

"Wait! That is all I do. Wait, he says! I told you, if you don't want to marry me now, fine—but don't get yourself killed. Ohhh, Frost, please," she leaned forward, touching his hand, squeezing his fingers, "can't you ever learn to deal with the idea of someone loving you, worrying about you?"

"Yeah," Frost said, then stood up and walked toward the small wall divider separating the dinette from the kitchen. Turning, he said, "I can deal with it just fine. But how we gonna live, huh? Tell me that."

Then, fumbling in his shirt pocket for his cigarettes, he saw them on the table, and walked over beside Bess, reached down and took a Camel from the half-dead pack. He lit it with his Zippo. His left shirt cuff was starting to come down and he rolled it back up. Sitting still, Bess took his hand, looking up at him.

"I make—"

"I know what you make," Frost said. "I can do one thing only—because of this a little," and he gestured roughly toward the eyepatch, "and because of what I am. What? You want me to make four bucks an hour as a bank guard or something while you pull down thirty or forty thousand a year and expenses? Uh-uh."

"But what can you—"

"I can keep working until something big comes along and I can get a stake, then do something with it."

"Or is it that you just like playing soldier?" Bess said, her voice low, starting to crack.

Dropping into a crouch, the Camel hanging from his lips on the left side of his mouth, he grabbed her by both arms, turned her around and stared at her.

"What the hell else am I supposed to do? Diablo Security really proved to be a safe job, didn't it? I almost really bought it back there in France with the Nazis. What, be a security man all the time? For how much money, huh?"

"When you were a little boy," she said, standing and walking away from him, her hands shaking as she smoothed her skirt down, "didn't you ever decide what you wanted to do for a living?"

"I told you about that," he said, walking to the opposite end of the room. "I was raised to be a soldier. It's not my fault I'm a Goddamned anachronism these days. I trained to be a teacher—fine. Work in the inner cities and you just call yourself a teacher—you're a blasted soldier without a gun, and God help you if you defend yourself. I almost killed that kid who was raping that black teacher. Spend my life in the slammer just to earn a two-bit living? No!"

"But—"

"But what?" Frost said.

"But, isn't there something else?"

"I'm trapped, and I built the trap myself. I can't teach anyplace better than where I did years back without going back to school myself. How do I pay for that? Where do I get the patience, huh? I can't be a career military man in anybody's army with the eye gone. Remember Uncle Sam—kiss off, Captain Frost. Sorry you're injured."

"What about—well, disability?"

"I got it coming; I don't take it. They wanted to do something for me, they could've let me stay in the Army. They can take their money and shove it. No—if I keep up what I'm doing, I'll get in on something."

"You just want to fight, that's all," she said, raising her voice.

"Communists? Two-bit dictators? Yeah, I want

to fight them." Then lowering his voice, Frost said, "I don't want to fight you."

"Why – you afraid I'll leave you. Like your mother left your father?"

Frost just looked at her, then very quietly, lighting another cigarette, said, "Yeah," and turned and walked around the divider toward the kitchen. He picked up the bottle of Seagrams and poured three fingers into a glass he found in the drainboard . . .

They talked for a while longer, without further arguing. "Am I cooking any better?" she finally asked him.

"Yeah," he grunted. "You're comin' along. Come here."

Frost sat on the couch, Bess on a small straight-backed chair opposite him. She stood up and walked around the table, reaching out her hand. Frost took it and pulled her down to his lap, holding her there in his arms. "Why do we fight?" she asked, her voice soft.

"Practicing for when we get married sometime, maybe," Frost said.

"Bullshit!"

"You shouldn't talk dirty," he told her.

"What are you going to do about it?" she said, a smile crossing her lips and making small dimple-like lines at the corners of her mouth.

"I don't wanna get into any of that kinky stuff – shut up and kiss me," Frost said.

He hooked his left arm behind her neck, leaning her back deeper into his arms, his mouth going down on hers, their lips touching for the briefest of time, then parting.

"What are you doing?" she asked, her voice in a whisper. Frost stared at her, then touched the fingers of his right hand to her mouth, tracing the smile he found there.

"What are you doing?" she asked again.

Frost put his fingers to her lips, and she kissed them as he said, "I'm looking at you — see I've got to look at you, so I'll have something to remember later when I'm gone. The details — like which dimple is bigger, you know, stuff like that."

"Just think what you could have done with dialogue like that in a war movie," she laughed.

"Shut up," Frost said.

"Make me," she smiled.

Frost looked at her a moment, smiling, then, shrugging his shoulders, said, "Okay."

As Bess's lips started to part, Frost touched them with his, her arms encircling his neck. His right hand touched at her left breast, felt the subtle movement of her breathing, then slipped down to her waist, ran along the flanks of her thighs and stopped just above her knees. His fingers explored under the hem of her dress, then ran up the way they had come. He felt the silky smoothness of her stockings as his fingers moved along her thighs, then stopped, again at her waist. She moved in his arms as he pulled the panties and the pantyhose down and found the triangle of hair at her crotch. His fingers toyed with it a moment, and then found the moist heat there as they explored inside her.

Her head cocked back, her eyes closed, the lids fluttered slightly as his fingers played with her. After a while he bent and kissed her mouth again.

161

Bess sighed audibly, her breathing rapid. The smile frown lines on his lightly stubbled cheeks knitted into a grin and he started to raise her in his arms, at the same time trying to stand. The thought crossed his mind that in the movies it always looked so easy – the guy just snatched the girl up into his arms as though she were as light as a feather.

"You been eatin' rocks?" Frost whispered in her ear as he got to his feet, Bess cuddled in his arms.

"Hmmm," was all she said, her eyes smiling, her lips in a pale enigmatic curve.

Frost carried her to the bedroom and set her on the quilt covered double bed. Kicking off his shoes and dropping his pants – "The hell with the rest," he thought – he sat on the bed beside her. His hands massaged at her thighs, her body moving under his fingers. Pushing up the skirt of her dress past her hips, then pulling her underwear down past her ankles and throwing it into the corner of the room, he stretched out on the bed beside her.

His fingers playing with her, he kissed her mouth and after a moment slipped on top of her, coming between the heat of her legs. He could feel her hands gliding down along his chest, touching him, then holding him, feel her guiding him into her. Frost could feel himself growing inside her, hear the little sucking sounds of her flesh against his, feel her lips touching his cheek. His right hand under her bare rear end, he arched her up toward him.

He buried his face in her neck, the desire Frost had had for her for the many months they'd been apart exploding inside of her. He heard her voice

sounding warm and happy but somehow far away —
as though she were dreaming — whispering, her lips
touching his cheek, "I love you, Frost."

Frost whispered, "I know."

They slept in each other's arms through the night,
and in the morning made love once again, slowly —
it would be the last chance before Frost left again
for Paris, they thought. In mid morning, Bess had
suggested that they go riding. "What — horses?"
Frost asked incredulously.

"No — grapefruit! Of course horses, Frost. What'd
you think I meant?"

"Well —"

"Come on — fresh air, the whole shot. Come on,
huh?" Frost agreed then against, he felt, his better
judgment. Bess had a car, and Frost leaned back,
his eye closed as she wove the little MGB, top down,
through the morning traffic and into the country.
Frost's things were already stowed in the car. They
would not return to the apartment.

"Why is your eye closed," she asked, the sound
of her shifting into a lower gear unmistakable to Frost.

"I can't bear to watch — got a weak heart, you
know."

"Agh," she grunted, and Frost heard her wrenching at the gearbox again.

In less than a half hour, they were grinding to a
gravel chewing stop beside a bright red painted barn.

"This the horse place?" Frost said.

"They call it a stable," Bess said, climbing out
from behind the wheel. As Frost got out he watched
her — white blouse under a heavy, gray bulky knit sweater. There was something funny about the sleeves, he

163

noted—they didn't come all the way down to her wrists. You could still see the French cuffs of the blouse—and the sleeves got awfully wide at the end. He guessed the sweater was designed that way. She wore tight fitting black pants and high black riding boots.

"Safe to leave your purse in the car?" Frost shouted after her as she walked briskly around the barn.

"Yeah—come on, stick-in-the-mud!"

Frost shrugged his shoulders and followed her.

After a few minutes the horses were saddled and a guy who looked like an extra in a movie about Ireland was standing back by the barn with the two animals. Bess walked over to a large brown horse—Frost remembered her calling it a bay mare—and mounted easily. "This one's for you," she said.

He crunched across the gravel and cinders and walked up to the large gray horse. "Why's my saddle different than yours?" he said.

"Oh, come on Frost. I'm riding English, I figured you'd like Western—that's all."

"What's his name," Frost said, looking at Bess and gesturing to the horse.

"Her name is Pokey—sounds like she's made for you. Come on—mount up."

Frost eyed the Irish looking guy—a groom Bess had called him—and the man stepped back, releasing the stirrup he'd held to help Frost aboard. "I'll do okay," Frost said, forcing confidence into his voice and taking the reins in his left hand. He put his right hand on the saddle horn and his left foot in the stirrup. As he started to mount, the horse started to move and the groom came forward and quieted

164

the animal. As Frost got into the saddle, Bess said, "You really weren't kidding—you don't know how to ride!"

As Frost squirmed to get comfortable in the saddle, he looked across at Bess. "If God had meant man to get around on four legs, he would have put four socks in a pair!"

As Bess was already starting down the trail Frost looked at the reins in his hands. The groom said, "Sir, just give her her head and she'll follow Miss Stallmann's horse, Eyepatch."

Frost held the reins a moment, looked down at the man and said, "Eyepatch—that's a funny name for the horse."

"I wouldn't know, Sir," the man said, his accent sounding more Scottish to Frost than Irish. "Miss Stallman used to call her Brownie, then after she returned from Switzerland she changed the name of the horse." Frost looked along the trail—Bess had been in Switzerland with him.

"Eyepatch, huh," Frost muttered under his breath, then kicked his heels into the horse's sides and held on to the saddle horn as the horse started along the trail.

Bess slowed her horse after a few minutes and Frost's animal caught up easily. Then they rode side-by-side for a half-hour until Bess had called for a rest.

They left the horses tied to a log in the bare woods and walked a short distance from the trail, Frost smoking, Bess talking. "When will you be back, Frost?" she finally asked.

"As soon as I can."

165

"What's after this job?" she asked.

"I think I might have a handle on an arms deal—all legitimate and everything. Back stateside for overseas shipment. Just bringing together a few people I know for a percent of a percentage—should be about sixty-four thousand bucks if it comes off."

Looking at him—Frost watched the sunlight on her face—she said, "I thought you said once that most people in the arms business were a bunch of window-shoppers."

"Yeah, well, I think this is different," he said, then throwing the cigarette down and crushing it under his heel, he took her in his arms.

He kissed her. "You taste good in the cold."

He took his arms from her and Bess turned away, walked a few paces, then turned back to face him. "I'm a fool—I'm gonna wait for you. But Frost, if you get killed, so help me I'll—"

In two short strides Frost was beside her, his arms around her waist, his mouth crushing hers. Frost whispered beside her ear and Bess, her lips against his cheek said, "What did you say, Frost?"

"I said thank you—I wanted you to."

Two hours later, Frost was flying by commercial jet across the English Channel.

Chapter Fourteen

The mists were rolling off the damp bogs and all but obscured the ground and the bases of the large tree trunks dotting the woods. A man was at the edge of the mists, and Frost, from his perch on a broad limb over the rough track bisecting the woods, could make out no details. He tried concentrating on the man, more than necessary, he realized, but his face itched—he was allergic to camouflage stick and his face was painted in it. His legs aching from the crouch he was in, Frost slowly, soundlessly, moved them and stretched himself out on the limb, his hands in fingerless gloves pressed against the dank treebark. His eye, under the brim of the camouflage crusher hat he wore, never once left the figure at the edge of the

167

small clearing to the side of the track. Frost carried no rifle, his only weapons his Metalifed Browning High Power 9mm, his Gerber MkI boot knife and a borrowed Heckler & Koch flare pistol—the latter not really a weapon at all, but was a backup for signalling to Fouchard and his Sûreté counter-terrorist team should the small radio he carried in a pouch strapped to his chest under his camouflage field jacket be lost or prove inoperable. Two starburst flares would be a signal to move in.

As Frost watched the figure leave the edge of the clearing and cross into the mists, he wished silently for a cigarette, or that, like many of the men in his profession, he liked to chew snuff or tobacco. He thought back a moment to an old friend back in the States—George Dreyer, a tough little guy now in his eighties. The man had always tried getting Frost to try snuff—Copenhagen—and Frost's eternal response had been negative.

The figure Frost had been watching was lost to him now in the swirling pre-dawn mists, but he knew the man had to still be somewhere in the clearing. The diamonds were almost directly under Frost and the tree limb he occupied—ten million dollars in diamonds of five to eight carats. A heavy package, Frost recalled, having watched as—per instructions of the terrorists—a uniformed French policeman placed them there an hour earlier.

As the figure re-emerged for a moment, then was swallowed once again by the mists, Frost shifted position on the tree limb—only more uncomfortably this time. He felt that if he didn't urinate in the next few minutes he'd die of kidney failure.

And he could see the figure again. The thought crossed his mind that he could always do like Robin Hood and jump from the tree limb—after all, he was wearing green—and just hold his knife to the figure's throat. He could say, "All right, where's Balsam—talk or I'll slit your throat from ear to ear." But Frost shelved the idea. Today's terrorists were a dedicated lot and all Frost would likely wind up with was a terrorist with his throat whacked instead of information. He decided to try to follow the plan and follow the terrorist, then see what developed.

Frost could see the figure more clearly now—it was a man, unmistakably. There were so many women in terrorist activity these days, Frost reflected, it was hard to be sure.

The man carried a small, almost pistol-sized submachine gun in a sling from his right shoulder. He wore dark clothes—not camouflaged—and something like combat boots. Frost watched as the man walked directly beneath him, straight to the package of diamonds. Frost resented that perhaps more than anything—the terrorist expected the diamonds to be there, expected there to be no trap—expected humble compliance from the people he was blackmailing with the threat of death or destruction. To Frost, this was the most intolerable thing in any terrorist-related activity. The goody-goody people of the world gave in to the terrorist demands to the point where any damned fool, Frost thought, could get a bomb or submachine gun and hold someone somewhere hostage and make himself an international celebrity.

The man still almost directly beneath him stopped, bent over, and hefted the packet of diamonds in his left hand. Then he clutched it under his arm. Unhurriedly, he started walking back through the mists, across the rough track of road and into the fog-covered clearing.

Shaking his head, Frost scanned the area as best he could, saw no other sign of human life besides himself and the terrorist kidnapper. Then, coming up into a crouch, he jumped to the ground, landed in a crouch again, dusted off his semi-gloved hands. Before starting after the man, Frost turned into the bushes near the tree trunk, pulled off his right glove and urinated. A smile crossing his lips as he pulled up the zipper, Frost put back his glove and took off at a slow, even jog trot across the track and into the clearing. He stayed near the tree line and went around the open area rather than through it. His legs still ached, and the cuts itched a little, a sign they were on the mend, but the fresh bandages that had been applied that afternoon by the Army Doctor Fouchard had supplied weren't uncomfortable. His left shoulder ached a little from the dampness, the wounds there just bloody grazes that had not damaged muscle or bone.

As Frost reached the far edge of the clearing, he could just barely make out the man he was tracking, as his quarry led Frost to the higher ground and cut up through the tree line, he kept parallel and slightly behind. For all his seemingly casual attitude, Frost decided, the man he followed was reasonably good in the woods. He moved virtually as soundlessly as Frost himself, sticking to as much open space as possible so—he turned and looked over his shoulder incessantly, Frost thought—he could see if he were being followed.

But Frost had expected tougher. The man was certainly not sticking to camouflage and concealment. He was just moving through the woods— more like a skilled deerhunter would travel than a man who himself might be stalked by other men.

"Thank God for small favors," Frost muttered to himself, then on impulse glanced over his own shoulder. He thought he spotted someone ducking behind a stand of close-together pines. There was no time, Frost realized, to wait and see if he too were being followed—the time that that would take would lose him the man with the ransom.

Frost reached the top of the hill and scanned the open country before him. He could see his man clearly, staying near the tree line and obviously heading toward a dirt road at the far side of the open ground. Shaking his head, Frost headed in the opposite direction laterally, staying below the brow of the hill until he reached the opposite tree line, then just inside the pines followed his quarry along a parallel line. He wanted to get up even with the man just in case there was a car waiting along the dirt road, so he ran as best he could in the heavy underbrush by the edge of the tree line and the field.

Glancing back over his shoulder again, Frost was sure this time: someone was following him. Looking forward, he could see, across the hundred or so yards of open field on the opposite tree line, the man with the ransom, coming up to the dirt road, looking both ways as though he were crossing a downtown street, then crossing it, going on along the tree line.

As Frost reached the road, he dropped down in the ditch alongside, watched his man over the rim, then almost diving, went across the road, coming down in the opposite ditch. Again, Frost hugged the opposite tree line, only taking his eye from his quarry to occasionally look behind him and confirm that he too was still being followed.

The sun was starting to rise now, the mists on the field between Frost and his man beginning to evaporate. There was another dirt road less than a half-mile ahead and Frost, less than fifty yards behind his quarry, watched as the man homed right toward it. And, minutes later, as the terrorist reached the road, Frost observed the man stuffing the small SMG he carried under his coat, then turning and walking along the side of the road as though he were out for a casual stroll.

Frost reached the road, then staying on the near side behind his man—he didn't dare cross in open view—he followed, hugging the tree line until he had to cross the open field for a hundred yards. He made a dash across the open ground, not stopping to catch his breath until he had the cover of the trees again. Approaching the road, he could see his quarry, perhaps two hundred yards off, crossing the dirt road finally and cutting through another wooded area. Frost crossed the road himself, catching sight again of whoever it was that was following him. Making another dash along the opposite tree line, he stopped about fifty yards away from where

172

his quarry had entered the woods. Moving then as silently as he could Frost flanked the man, keeping him in sight as they both approached another dirt road. Frost checked his watch. He had been following the man for more than an hour now.

Shaking his head—he wished the man would stop —Frost watched as the terrorist turned up the dirt road and crossed it, then turned up a smaller road running—it appeared—along the far side of the woods.

Frost cut along the tree line as fast as he could, then reached the edge of the woods. The road was more of a drive, an access road, and at its end a rather large, old farmhouse. On a hunch, Frost kept concealed, watching as the man carrying the ransom under his arm like a loaf of bread headed up the access road and turned in toward the house.

Frost glanced behind him—he'd heard something. Taking a last quick look, he watched as the man with the ten million dollars in diamonds entered the farmhouse. Frost could see smoke coming from the chimney. He realized he had a more immediate problem now—taking out whoever was following him. Quickly, as he moved deeper into the trees away from the access road, Frost mentally ticked off the possibilities. If Fouchard didn't trust him, the man could be from the Sûreté. But, Frost decided, then why was he here to begin with, if Fouchard could use one of his own men for that? Likely, Frost decided, whoever was following him was Nazi—perhaps a backup man if the terrorists holding Balsam were in fact with the Party. If the people holding Balsam weren't Nazis—as everything now

173

seemed to indicate — then the Nazis might be interested in snatching Balsam and the ransom.

Frost stopped, falling soundlessly to the ground, spreadeagling his body to show the lowest possible profile above the ground. He could see who was following him, less than fifty yards from him — the girl he had known as Sheila Balsam, the Mossad Agent Marita Litski.

The dark hair was covered with a black bandanna, black like the rest of the clothes she wore. Her face was camouflage-sticked — like Frost's — but he could almost imagine the green eyes, bright and intense — a lot like Bess's.

Rather than standing up and walking over and saying hello, Frost thought that it would be better to surprise her — and safer. He inched across the ground, moving quickly when the cover and surface permitted, slowing when she turned to look his way, or when the dull winter grass was thinner around him. He narrowed the distance to ten yards, waiting by a deadfall tree, calming himself, for the final run. She was turning around more often now, perhaps having heard something, Frost thought, but he couldn't be sure.

He drummed the fingers of his left hand against the handle of the Gerber knife, then snatched instead the Browning 9mm from the diagonal Jerry Rig shoulder holster under his field jacket. He'd coated the pistol's usual gleaming surface with an easily removable field bluing, the black rubber Pachmayr grips grips settling well in his right hand.

Pushing himself up to his feet, he took off toward Marita Litski in a dead run. Frost had crossed half the ten yard distance separating them before she turned, a submachine gun in her hands, the muzzle coming on line with him. Frost leaped, sailing into her and knocking her back, just then realizing the girl had been perched on the edge of a small rise. Frost and the girl in his arms now toppled over the edge, rolling down the embankment, coming to rest hard against a tree trunk a dozen or more feet below.

"What—" the girl was breathing hard, "—the hell—"

Frost cut her off, wrestling the Uzi from her hands and knocking her back against the tree trunk, then falling to a sitting position himself, his wind gone.

"So go ahead and now shoot me!" she said, her face tight with anger, her eyes rivetted to Frost's right hand. He looked down and noticed the Browning still in his grasp.

"Relax," Frost grunted, then leaned back on his elbows, resting his pistol and the SMG he'd snatched from her on the ground beside him. The girl was in motion before he could get out of the way, her hands going for his throat, her knee smashing against his crotch.

Frost hooked his left arm over her hands and rolled to the right, breaking her chokehold on his neck, rolling back and slamming his elbow into the side of her neck. Starting to his feet after her, Frost stopped. Somehow—he couldn't figure from where —a knife had appeared in her right hand.

Some people were exceedingly good with knives, Frost thought—and apparently Marita Litski was one of them.

"Come on, Nazi pig," she snarled.

As Frost dodged her first lunge, he stammered, "Hey, who you callin' a Nazi — want to see the scars, kid?"

"Liar!" she shouted, almost spitting the word in his face. She started for him with the knife again and Frost sidestepped, caught her feet with his left foot and she started down. Turning on his right heel, Frost crossed his body with his left fist, hooking the girl not too gently on the jaw and spilling her back a yard or so up the slope.

The knife was gone from her hand, and as Frost started toward her, she started to get up, then slumped back, rubbing her jaw. She started up again, and Frost fell onto her, pinning her to the ground, his right leg twisted in front of him to guard against her giving him a knee in the crotch.

"Now take it easy," Frost said, bracing his elbow against her left arm, brushing half-rotted leaves from her hair — now loose, the bandanna gone — with his fingers. "I think we're on the same side — I'm tailing the guy who picked up the ransom to try and get Doctor Balsam back — you too?"

"Liar!" she half screamed.

Frost, looking at her intently, said "Knock it off with the noise, okay? Otherwise, this time I'll really deck you. Got me?"

He felt her muscles relaxing, and started to release his grip, then ducked back as her right hand came at him with a small, stubby-bladed knife. With his right fist, Frost back handed her knife hand at the wrist, the knife flying from her fingers. On the recovery swing, Frost clipped her in the jaw, then sat back. The girl Mossad agent, Marita, lay there, and if she weren't unconscious, Frost decided, she was the world's best actress.

Leaning over her and rolling back her eyelids slightly, he satisfied himself that she was out. Then stubbing a cigarette between his lips and lighting it with his Zippo, he worked his way back down the small rise to the edge of the tree line, catching up his pistol and her SMG as he went.

The fire was still going in the farmhouse – the smoke from the chimney was black against the sky's blue, the sun now well-risen. Frost worked his way back up toward where the girl lay, searched the bushes and found her knives – one an A. G. Russell Sting IA, the all stainless steel double-edged boot knife with finger-grooved handle portion but no actual handle slabs; the other, the knife she'd hauled out last, a knife Frost's friend Chris McLoughlin touted. Chris, with his inimitable flair for naming things, called it the "Dead Ringer." You put the blade on your middle finger like a ring, then used it like a gambler's push dagger or a inside-the-palm dagger." Frost put both knives on the ground beside her 9mm UZI SMG, waiting for Marita to awaken.

Frost had finished his first cigarette and started a second when he saw her eyelids flutter. He said, "Now, Marita, I was a gentleman – I didn't search you. I'm sure you've got a handgun somewhere under your clothes. Go for it and I'll kill you. So listen."

Pushing herself up on one elbow, the girl stared at him, saying nothing. Frost told her the truth – an encapsulated version of everything from his

177

capture by the Nazis and his escape to being re-
cruited by Fouchard to trail the terrorist who picked
up the ransom. He left out any mention of Bess.

"You expect me to believe that — you're crazy."

"Fine," Frost droned, "then I'll shoot you."

"Hah!" she said, half-laughing. "Go ahead —
alert everybody in the house down there that we're
out here."

"If I shoot you," Frost reminded her, "*we* will
no longer be out here — only I will. What do you
want?"

"A truce then," she said, the reluctance in her
voice obvious.

"Good." Frost stubbed out his cigarette beside
his foot and automatically field stripped it. "Then
let's get the hell down to the house and stop all
this foolishness. I'll keep this — you got spare ammo?"

Frost gestured with the UZI. The girl, glaring
at him, lifted and dropped the small musette-like
bag crossing her shoulders, saying, "Here — four spare
thirty's."

"Terrific — let's go." Frost got to his feet — his
legs were stiffening up again — and started into the
trees. In a moment, he heard the girl behind him.

After a few minutes, they were back at the tree
line, this time less than fifty yards from the house,
a white-painted American type stock fence ten
yards from the edge of the trees.

"You got a pistol then?" Frost asked, contin-
uing the conversation they'd had several hundred
yards back.

"Yes," she said, then reached under her black
field jacket — the bandanna was back in place on

178

her head, tied at the nape of her neck – and produced a Walther PPK. Frost glanced at the muzzle. It was a .22, a favorite with Israeli security people.

"You don't have a silencer for that, do you?" Frost asked.

The girl reached under her coat again. This time her hand reappeared with a Sionics-appearing suppressor, fitting it over the longer than average barrel of the Walther.

"What," Frost asked absently. "A PPK slide on a PP frame with the original longer PP barrel."

"More or less," Marita answered noncommitally.

"Any guards come up and it requires shooting, you're on," Frost told her. "Come on."

Frost started out of the tree cover and ran in a low crouch toward the fence, stopping beside a vertical support and going flat. In less than a minute the girl was beside him at the next post.

Frost, using hand signals, told the girl to follow his lead, taking the same route toward the house that he used. She merely nodded, her eyes almost bored looking, Frost thought. He started for the house, running in a low crouch and keeping near the fence line as long as he could.

There was a bricked-up, low-rising covered well – like something he would have expected to see in the American southeast – and Frost took cover behind it. The girl joined him a moment later. "You see any guards?" he whispered.

"Nothing. Maybe they've gone."

"If they got out of here," Frost said, "they're invisible. The only time I didn't have at least half an eye on this place was during the couple of minutes we were fighting back there — and I would have heard any vehicles going down the road."

"Maybe then," she said, "they just do not expect trouble — that would be stupid."

"Yeah — well. Let's find out."

Frost pushed himself up into a crouch again, then took off in a run from the well toward the side of the farmhouse, dropping down just under a window on the near side by the road.

The girl was beside him again. Holding his finger to his lips, Frost raised his head slightly. He didn't dare look inside the house, but he tried listening. From inside, he heard voices, some laughter — and one of the voices was that of Professor Balsam. Frost could not make out the words.

He put his lips to Marita's ear, "Heard Balsam — sounds okay. Others in there too. Let's go." Then, pointing to himself, he whispered, "Front door." And then, to Marita, "Back. Count to twenty and go."

Frost started up.

In mid-stride, he stopped, turned his eye toward the dirt access road, then shouted, "Marita!" But already there was the rattle of submachine gun fire. And the only face Frost recognized among the occupants pouring out of the four cars was Liebling, the Nazi.

Chapter Fifteen

The gunfire from the access road seemed to have awakened the occupants of the house as well, Frost thought, for as he dove toward Marita to bring her down, the window over his head shattered outward. Above them roared the light steady cracking of a light caliber assault rifle. As Frost pushed Marita to the ground, the wooden slats of the house just over his head started splintering, metal jacketed submachine gun bullets ripping into the outside wall from the cars by the road.

The girl looked up at Frost—"What do we do, Hank?"

"What you mean we . . . " Frost started, the old joke the first thing that came to mind. Then, "Into the house—out here we're dead."

As the assault rifle reached out the window above him again, Frost grabbed at it with his gloved left palm, swatting the gun away and shoving the muzzle of the girl's Uzi in through the window, then diving in after it. Frost hit the floor of the house and went into a roll. As he started to bring the gun's muzzle on line to fire—out of the corner of his eye seeing Marita coming in the window now too—he heard Professor Balsam shouting at the top of his voice, "Wait—we are all friends—no shooting."

Frost's finger against the Uzi's trigger, his eye tracked toward the sound of the voice. Half behind a table but wholly visible, he could see Balsam, looking just as Frost had last seen him—except for the left hand, swathed in bandages and stained with blood.

"What the hell is going on here," Frost said in a low voice. "We are all friends?"

Frost caught sight of Marita, the silenced Walther in her right fist, the Russell Sting knife in her left. her legs apart, knees flexed, ready to spring like a cat.

"I can explain, Captain Frost—my friend," Balsam said, his voice more normal now, a smile on his lips.

The gunfire from the road was quiet now, Frost noticed. Still crouched on the floor, the Uzi in his hands, he said, "Let me tell you—these guys are some kind of group of anti-Nazi ideologues. You knew you were terminally ill with cancer, so you decided to get up a little fund raiser for the gang here—right?"

"That is more or less the spirit of the thing, Captain Frost—a parting gift, so to speak. Surely, to

182

fight such animals as those," – and Balsam gestured toward the road – "no personal sacrifice is too great."

"What about the French motorcycle cops who got killed, what about the chauffeur who got beheaded when we hit the truck," Frost rasped, his voice getting uncontrollable.

"These people here," Balsam gestured to the people in the house, "are amateurs – they know nothing of violence. And, in their attempt to execute the plan they failed and took innocent lives. But how many innocent lives will these diamonds save?"

Frost looked at Balsam, at the crowd of fresh faced young kids assembled in the room. Frost said, "Aren't you and your friends getting as bad as what you're fighting out there?" As Frost started to say something else, he caught sight of Marita again, the muzzle of the silenced Walther starting to swing in an unmistakable plane with Professor Balsam's head. Dropping the Uzi from his hands, Frost dove toward her, the pistol flying from her grasp.

"Don't try to stop me," she screamed, over and over. "If word of what this fool has done gets to the world press, the cause of the Jewish people will be set back decades – my God."

Frost determined, quickly, that Marita was in hysterics. He slapped her face, once, then once again, hard. She started to cry and stopped screaming. The gunfire from outside was starting up again and Frost, looking over his shoulder at Balsam, said very quietly, "She's right."

A window blew out over Frost's head and he pushed himself and the girl down on the floor. As one of the youngsters Balsam had assembled there

183

started for Frost's borrowed Uzi, the Browning flashed in Frost's right fist and he rasped, "Touch it kid and you're dead—understand English?"

The "kid"—a girl Frost noticed as he got a better look at the face—smiled embarrassedly and looked at him, saying, "*Oui, Monsieur.*"

Frost thought that he half expected her to curtsey.

Dragging Marita with him, Frost started across the floor, catching up the Uzi and the girl's Walther and stopping behind the heavy oak table next to Balsam. None from inside the house was returning fire to the Nazis on the roadside, all just staring at Frost, Marita and Dr. Balsam.

"Do you think we should shoot back—hmm," Frost said, trying for all the sarcasm he could put into his voice.

The young men and women in the house—as if of one mind, suddenly picked up their arms—a collection of mismatched automatic weapons and assault rifles—and returned to the windows, opening fire toward the road.

Marita quieting down beside him now, Frost turned back to Balsam, trying to avoid glancing down at the man's hand—what was left of it. "Why?"

"You know why, my friend," Balsam said, still smiling.

"No, but—why this way."

"Very simple. My plan was designed to accomplish two goals—you must believe that no one was supposed to get hurt. If the Nazis had not attacked at the hotel that morning, there would have been no French motorcycle police, and the car we drove would have been more easily stopped and the chauffeur would not have been killed. We felt—all of us—that my kidnapping would dramatize to the world what a real threat the Nazis were—to everyone. Not just—like you said on the airplane—a bunch of crazies no one takes seriously. And to get money—these young people must be able to buy guns if necessary to fight the Nazi threat, to buy publicity, to organize. It would pay for assassinations of the Nazi leaders—stop another holocaust before it can begin."

Balsam was still smiling, and Frost was beginning to think the man had gone insane.

"But Professor," Frost started, then shrugged his shoulders. Turning away and looking at Marita, her face inches from his, the camouflage paint now streaked with lines from her tears, he handed her the Walther pistol, butt first, saying, "Here—go kill some Nazis—the real ones are outside."

The girl looked at him a moment, forced a strange sort of smile and took the pistol, murmuring, "I'll be all right."

Frost only nodded, then left Balsam and followed the girl toward the front windows of the house, across the bullet-pocked living room floor, to where the heaviest fire from the road was coming.

As Frost reached the window, he handed Marita her Uzi, then taking his pistol started lobbing single rounds toward the cars, aiming for the nearest gas tank. Five rounds gone and one of his bullets connected, the gas tank of the nearest car—a Renault—going up in a ball of fire, the Nazis huddled behind it running. "Fire at them," Frost shouted, emptying his Browning at the men fleeing the flames.

Beside him, he heard one of the women defenders burst into tears. "They're burning," she screamed.

Frost fired until his pistol was empty, then grabbed an M-16 from a young boy beside him who wasn't using it. Frost picked up the firing, catching two more of the Nazis as they fled the flames of the burning car.

Handing the rifle back to the boy, Frost turned around and shouted across the room to Balsam. "If you're wondering right now if you did the right thing, Doc, I don't think so. See that girl over there," Frost pointed — rude he thought — to the girl who had cried when one of the Nazis out by the road had started running, his clothes on fire. "See her, Doc," Frost went on, the bitterness he felt obvious in his voice. "She's just a young girl, doesn't want to get or harm anybody — even Nazis. You're gonna make a stone killer out of her — maybe if they come for her mother in the middle of the night, but it hasn't come to that. You're preaching hate the same way they are. You ever listen to bigots talking to their kids — Nigger this, Jew that, Jap the other. Makes you want to puke, doesn't it. Well, consider yourself one of the club, Doc." Ignoring the gunfire over his head and around him, Frost figured then that he was quite probably going to die, so he lit a cigarette, glared at Balsam a moment, then stared down at the floor between his combat boots.

After a long minute, Frost heard someone shouting in English — he assumed for his benefit — "The police — they are coming."

Frost looked at the one who had cried out — a boy of about nineteen or twenty, then said to him,

186

"What the hell you so excited about the police coming for, kid. All they're gonna do is arrest you for murder, terrorism, extortion, and everything else they can invent a law for."

Frost turned back toward the window, stared out, glad that the dark Citroens coming down the road —flashing lights on the roofs—were the cars of the counter-terrorist squad. He couldn't make out Fouchard, but Frost knew the men were good.

The French police were armed with submachine guns, but there were nearly twice as many Nazis as police, Frost observed. Almost as soon as the police arrived they started falling back. "Come on —we can get 'em in a crossfire," Frost shouted, but there was little answering gunfire from inside the house. Throwing up his hands in disgust, Frost shouted to anyone who would listen, "Is there any way out of here—come on, somebody!"

Glancing over his shoulder and out the window, Frost could see at least a dozen of the Nazis starting to assemble behind the now burned-out Renault for—Frost guessed—an attack. And suddenly, the attack began. One of the Nazis, from a protected position behind the burned out Renault, began firing rifle grenades. Frost could hear the first grenade's explosion on the roof of the farmhouse, smoke now starting to filter down into the main floor living room where he and Balsam's defenders were holed up.

"There is an escape tunnel," the girl who had been crying hysterically a moment earlier shouted.

Moving toward her, keeping low to avoid flying glass and bullets whizzing overhead, Frost put his

187

hands on her shoulders, then saying, calmly, "Show me – quickly."

Signalling to Marita Litski, Frost followed the young girl across the living room – twice forcing her to keep down by putting his hand on her shoulder – toward the kitchen. Huge by American standards, the kitchen was sparsely furnished. "Help me move the table," she whispered. Frost and Marita each took a side and moved it toward the bare interior wall. Then she pulled away a braided blue rag rug; beneath it was a trap door. As she started to tug at the handle, Frost stepped beside her, saying, "Here, let me do that."

As he tugged at the brass handle that had been flush in the door with his left hand, Frost said to himself, "Why'd I open my big mouth." The door wouldn't budge. He put his right hand to it awkwardly beside his left, then braced himself and pulled. The door sprang up and Frost slid back onto his rear end on the floor.

"One crack and I'll hit you," Frost rasped to Marita Litski.

Just nodding her head, she said, "I wouldn't say a word."

Frost turned to the young girl from Balsam's group. "Where does this thing lead – you did check it out?"

"Ohh, of course – the tunnel goes back under the house and parallels the little road outside and ends near some rocks just by the edge of the trees."

"You got some flashlights," Frost asked.

"*Oui.*"

"Good," he said, "bring them and everybody

188

else. Leave about four or five by the windows to keep up some fire. Have them wait—" Frost made a quick mental calculation of the length of the tunnel and projected travel time "—and tell them to follow after five minutes. Don't bother closing up the tunnel."

The girl started running back into the living room, and Frost shouted after her, "Keep down."

"Do you think we'll make it out of here?" Marita asked.

"If the tunnel is like she says," Frost said, "then maybe. But once we're out of the tunnel, I don't know. We've got to hook up with Fouchard's people —and I don't think Balsam's scout group out there is gonna be too eager for that. Wait and see, all we can do."

Frost lit a cigarette while he and Marita waited for the young girl to return with Balsam and the rest of the defenders. Just as Frost was about to go and see where they were, the girl came into the kitchen, followed by close to a dozen of the young people.

"You left a few on the windows?" Frost asked as he started down into the tunnel.

"Yes—but let some of us go first—the tunnel splits into two dead-end passages halfway under the house—we know the right way."

Looking at her a moment, Frost nodded his head, grunted "Okay," and let the girl and five of the others get down into the tunnel first. As Marita started to follow then, Frost held her back. "We're goin' last kid." As the last of the Nazi-fighters passed, he added to Marita, "Just in case something goes wrong —at least we'll be in a position to do some shooting."

She nodded, giving what Frost thought was an overly melodramatic twist to the silencer on the .22 Walther she carried, then started down into the tunnel through the trap door.

The tunnel was narrow, not designed for massive use. Judging from the apparent age of the wooden shoring, Frost guessed the farmhouse had been used as a headquarters of some resistance group during the Second World War.

From the light of the many flashlights, Frost was able to keep Professor Balsam clearly in view just three people ahead of Marita. The light spilling down from the kitchen above the tunnel entrance soon began to dissipate, then vanished altogether as they rounded what Frost judged to be a small curve in the tunnel.

Frost took the borrowed flashlight in his hand and pressed the lens over the black face of his Omega, the effect momentarily heightening the glow of the luminous markings on the dial. He hoped that counting his paces and keeping track of the time would give him an indication of approximately where they would exit—just how close to the Nazi position outside.

After three minutes, the young people up ahead started bunching up slightly. They had been making good time Frost noted, and it was possible that already the lead people were at the exit. Frost, his back aching from stooping to walk below the tunnel ceiling, stopped a moment, showing his light ahead, catching Marita's arm as he did. The tunnel curved slightly just ahead and they edged slowly around the curve. Ahead, Frost could see a long shaft of daylight;

190

whatever blocked the tunnel exit now apparently moved aside.

As Frost started forward with Marita, he heard gunfire, screams, cries of pain. Muttering, "Fish in a damned barrel," he pressed Marita against a side wall. There was gunfire from the end of the tunnel now, some of the young people in front of them going down. His lips pressed to Marita's ear, Frost whispered, "Somebody up ahead is just spraying the tunnel with a submachine gun!"

Balsam had already exited the tunnel and so had the young man Frost had trailed from the bog — the one with the diamonds.

Then Frost heard a hissing noise. "Come on," he shouted, grabbing Marita by her arm and running with her back along the tunnel toward the curve. Glancing over his shoulder, he saw the end of the tunnel was almost blindingly bright, a wall of flame coming toward them, almost as if the tunnel were sucking the flames into itself.

"Flame thrower," Frost shouted as they hit the curve. He pushed Marita around it and back along the tunnel. Glancing behind him again, he could see the tongue of flame hitting the end of the tunnel before the curve and stopping, less than six feet from them. Frost and the girl stopped, both coughing from the smell of liquified petroleum.

"Gotta get back to the house," Frost rasped. "Those supports up ahead will have burned out." He started to look at his watch, realized that a gauge of the time would have been meaningless, then pushed Marita to get her to run faster.

Ahead of him, Frost could see the light from

the trap door leading up to the kitchen. And, as he ran closer, he could see the door already starting to close. He pushed ahead of Marita and threw himself up the wooden ladder leading up into the kitchen, the flat of his left forearm, his right hand, pressing against the trap door, forcing it back until he rolled through onto the floor. The Browning High Power was in his right fist as he landed in the kitchen.

"Wait — we thought it was the Nazis," the frightened voice intoned. Frost looked at the owner of the voice — a boy of eighteen or nineteen.

Standing up, Frost threw open the tunnel door and reached down to help Marita up.

"Who was holding the tunnel door," Marita asked.

"Him," Frost said, gesturing to the boy, "the anti-Hitler youth here." Starting toward the living room, Frost snapped to the boy, "Keep your gun trained on that tunnel door — don't shoot unless you see they aren't friendlies." And as Frost ran toward the front of the house with Marita, he realized bitterly that probably everyone else inside the tunnel when the flame-thrower was used was dead — hideously so.

The gunfire coming toward the house was sporadic; the gunfire from the few defenders by the living room windows even lighter. Crawling the last few feet across the broken glass and bullet splintered wooden floor, Frost peered out the center window. "Cease firing!" he shouted.

Two of the three remaining cars used by the Nazis were starting to pull away and Frost could see Balsam crammed into the lead vehicle. A man with a flame thrower unit on his back was running from the edge of the woods, a man beside him carrying the package of diamonds.

Frost took the Browning in his right hand, and using his left fist like a cup, rested both hands on the window sill and fired. The first round was a miss. He took a deep breath to steady himself and fired again. The bullet connected, striking the flame thrower pack near the hose connection. Frost, even across the fifty yards or so to the woods' edge, thought he heard the beginning of a scream, but if he did, it was drowned out in the whoosh of the flame-thrower bursting into a fireball of jellied gasoline, engulfing the man who'd worn it.

The third car started out. Frost noted that the man he'd seen a moment before with the package of diamonds had escaped. Now the Nazis really did have Balsam, too, Frost thought bitterly. "What a success . . . "

Chapter Sixteen

"We must first consider the one positive feature — Professor Balsam is indeed alive, and we know who has kidnapped him — this time he has really been kidnapped." Fouchard leaned back in his seat, raising his feet on the edge of his desk. Frost, watching him from the same seat he had occupied — how long ago — following the phony kidnapping, lit a cigarette.

"They will have taken him to their headquarters in the Bavarian Alps — he knows too much to trust to the fools they have here."

Frost glanced over his shoulder at Marita. "Did I miss something? What headquarters in the Bavarian Alps? The Nazis?"

"Yes," she said, her voice sounding tired.

"Perhaps," Fouchard interjected, "I can clarify things for you both. For a long time now we have known—by we I mean the European police and intelligence community—that the German Nazi Party has been using a castle in the Bavarian Alps—donated to them by one of their many rich supporters—as their European Headquarters. It is not a crime of itself to be a Nazi. There is nothing anyone can do about the castle. It is private property. But some contacts within Interpol have been feeding me bits and pieces of information about Professor Balsam's kidnapping. Small things—the landing of a private plane here, a car with a certain license plate going there. It is almost assured that the good doctor is a guest of the castle."

"Which means we've got to get him out," Marita said, "or kill him."

"Why are you so emphatic about that last part," Frost said, looking at her as she stood by the doorway.

"I cannot—"

"You had better, Mademoiselle," Fouchard said, his voice low, almost menacing Frost thought. "Or else you will not get any of the help I feel you will need immediately. I think I now know why Dr. Balsam is suddenly so important—but I want you to tell us."

Marita paced across the room, still dressed, like Frost, in the clothes she had worn during the attack on the farmhouse that morning. "All right—I'll tell you, but what I say does not leave this room. Agreed?"

Frost looked to Fouchard who nodded, then he

grunted his assent as well.

"We have known," she said, "for a long time of the existence of a group with cells throughout Europe which is training, to various degrees, to combat the neo-Nazi movement. And of course, we applaud their efforts. We had not known who their spiritual leader, so-to-speak, was. It appears it is Dr. Balsam. If the Nazis have him at their castle, their headquarters in Bavaria, it is for only one purpose."

"We are not sure he is there, Mademoiselle," Fouchard interrupted.

"No—and I know that unless there is proof, nothing official can be done by your government, Interpol, the German government—anyone. But if he is there—and I'm sure he is—then it can be for one purpose only," Marita repeated.

"I'll bite," Frost said.

Glaring at him, she said, "They will torture him, use drugs, whatever—they have sophisticated means at their disposal—to make him reveal the names, strengths, finances—all the details of the anti-Nazi movement in Europe. As it now stands, it seems the Nazis are on the brink of beginning a major terrorist movement of their own and such a group of dedicated anti-Nazis—however young and in-experienced—could become a major threat to them."

"Then back in the hotel," Frost mused, thinking out loud, "when they tried for Balsam their first intent was to kidnap him, and when my people and I cut down their numbers, they went to plan B—kill him."

"Yes," she said. "Apparently some time between

196

their attempt on Balsam's life at the Chicago airport and the attempt at the hotel here in Paris, they decided he was worth more alive than dead."

"It will be only a matter of time then," Fouchard said, staring at his ceiling, "until with drugs or under hypnosis Professor Balsam tells the Nazis everything he knows. Then, they will systematically assassinate everyone of importance in the movement and be able to carry out their plans for terrorist activity with greater confidence —"

"And boldness," Marita interrupted.

"What do we do," Frost asked, throwing the question to both Fouchard and the attractive young Mossad agent.

"I can call up a Commando strike with Israeli forces, but it would take at least twenty-four hours for it to be mounted — by then it might be too late," she said, sinking into a chair on the far wall.

"There is another alternative, Mademoiselle," Fouchard said, a smile crossing his lips.

"You count me in," Frost demanded. The girl leaned forward in her chair and Fouchard cocked his head back to stare at the ceiling again, then began to talk.

Chapter Seventeen

"I didn't think they still made planes like this," Frost shouted over the roar of the four props, the parachute pack still stuffed under his left arm.

Leaning close to Frost's ear Fouchard said, "They don't."

"That's what I thought," Frost said, stubbing out the butt of the Camel on the tarmac under his combat booted feet. He stared across the runway, the wind cold as it whipped up around him, the four props from the World War Two vintage bomber adding to its strength. The horizon was still dark, but Frost knew that as they left the small field and started to climb above the overcast cloud layers, they would find the sun, racing toward it as they made the comparatively short hop to Bavaria.

Marita Litski was standing a few yards closer to the plane than they, her clothes unchanged from the morning, the black pants tight inside the tops of her Corcoran jump boots.

"You need not go," Fouchard said.

Frost looked at him, saying, "What if everybody said that?"

"There are the volunteers from my counter-terrorist squad, the men from Mademoiselle Litski's Mossad detail—there are enough. You have the woman—Bess—back in London."

"I know," Frost said, lighting a cigarette, fighting the wind with his lighter.

"Then why do you do this?"

Frost looked at the man. Then, his face creasing into a half-hearted grin as he thought of Bess, Frost said, "If I knew the answer to that, my friend, I probably wouldn't be here—but back there in London."

"You are not a mercenary—I decided this," Fouchard said, clapping his right hand to Frost's left shoulder.

Smiling, Frost bent toward the shorter Fouchard and whispered, "Shhh—don't tell anyone."

Fouchard clapped him hard on the shoulder and Frost gave him a half-hearted salute as he started toward the plane, passing Marita Litski as he did, saying nothing.

As Frost seated himself along the starboard fuse-lage facing the cargo door, the sound of the engines grew in intensity. Marita Litski hopped aboard. As the French crewman closed the door, Frost could see Fouchard, now standing alone on the edge of the runway, his coat tight about him, his hat off against the wind.

Frost leaned back, studying the map by the beam of the Kel-Lite flashlight from his pack, mentally tracing the route they were beginning, memorizing the features of the drop zone. Marita Litski said nothing throughout the trip, all sixteen of the impromptu commando force sitting in comparative silence in the semi-darkness. Frost watched as each man tended to his weapons. Because the mission was impromptu, despite the identical Uzi submachine guns each carried, other personal weapons were widely different. Frost recognized a vintage Fairborne Sykes Commando Knife in the hands of one of the Frenchmen, a Randall Bear Bowie polished under the sleeve of one of the Mossad agents, his own Gerber Boot knife and the long-bladed Gerber he'd fished from his suitcase. It was one of the very early original Gerber MkIIs, the blade ultra slim and tapered like an hourglass. But it had always served him well.

He checked the Browning High Power 9mm, checked the spring pressure of the spare magazines pushing down the top cartridge under the feed lips against the follower stacked below at the base of the thirteen round magazine. Frost had eschewed an Uzi, taking a semi-automatic only CAR-15 and several thirty round magazines. He liked the weapon, and with rapid trigger action it was nearly as effective as a selective fire model—and burned considerably less ammo even in experienced hands. Fitted with the Colt scope, it made a serviceable long distance tool, and with the stock collapsed, it handled as well as a long barrel pistol. Frost gave the sling a check, then put the gun inside its drop case.

He checked the map again against his watch this time, fingering their approximate location—they should be crossing the border into Germany he knew. They were acting without the advice and consent of the West German government, but there was no choice.

The Germans were anti-Nazi, decidedly so, but there was no telling if their police or military had been infiltrated by the Nazis, and rather than risking blowing the operation, they were taking their chance with West German authorities. Parachuting into the country not far from the castle, then wearing the winter gear of West German forces, they would pretend to be a splintered West German unit on some type of patrol. For this reason, in addition to their own weapons, each man—Marita would be disguised as one—had a set of West German field gear, including a Walther Pl—the post war alloy-frame version of the P-38. Frost's own gun was given him by Fouchard—a loan, just in case, the man had said. It was a stubby barrelled P-38K with a Walther Supersonic silencer attachment—a unit favored by West German counter-terrorist units.

Captain Karkov of the Mossad broke the silence. "We should be nearing the drop point—why don't we gear up."

Frost, like the others, nodded, starting to pull the West German winter gear on over his own clothes. He'd changed to standard fatigues with thermal underwear and a crew neck sweater underneath before leaving. Without being told, each of them started getting up, some already hooking up to the static line before the red light went on. Karkov would be jump master.

One of the French crewmen came back and opened the hatchway. Frost leaned out, the cold biting at his skin. He pulled the toque down over his face. Glancing over his shoulder, he saw the green light, then heard Karkov shout, "Contaigne — go," and one of Fouchard's counter-terrorist team dove through the hatch, the tension on his static line building, then dissipating as below and to port side they could see his white chute opening above the snow-field below the shadowy silhouette of the plane itself. "Marita!" And Marita dove out. On impulse, Frost unclipped his static line and snapped it ahead of Beltzer — the Mossad man up next. "Me," Frost rasped to Karkov.

Karkov, his face twisted against the cold and wind, shouted, "Frost!" Frost nodded and dove.

The air, even beneath his protective clothing, was bitter cold, the silence suddenly — except for the rush of air around him — terrifying. He scanned the ground below him for sign of Marita, thought he could still see her chute.

Frost felt the jerk as the static line went taut, but he kept falling. A curse came to his lips as he craned his neck above him — the static line had pulled out and his chute had not opened. Frost spread his arms, trying to break his rate of descent, his mind racing against the watch on his wrist, the sweep second hand of the Omega seeming to move maddeningly to complete its 360 degree arc, the ground below him coming closer — sickeningly, perceptibly, inevitably.

202

He pulled the cord for the auxiliary chute on his chest and nothing happened. He had checked the chute himself, let it out of his sight for only a moment when Karkov had been in the ready room— Karkov! Frost's hands groped to the Gerber knife under his white gear, finding the butt of the boot knife and wrenching it free of the holster. The ground was racing up too fast—at the back of his mind Frost knew he wouldn't make it, but his hands acted independently of the despair in his heart and hacked at the packing closure for the auxiliary chute on his chest. He looked down to the chute, forcing himself with all his will to ignore the ground racing up to crush him. If he had a prayer, it was to cut the packing away and manually withdraw the chute. But one slip of the knife would puncture the chute and it would be useless—it would just be a ready-made shroud when he impacted against the ground.

Using the spear point tip of the Gerber, he had the packing half cut. Then he glanced down to the ground and began to tremble. Looking back to the packing he hacked at it more savagely, in his mind counting the seconds he had left, despair now telling him that even if he got the chute opened, it would be too late to break his rate of descent—perhaps it wouldn't open? Already—the knife clenched in his teeth—his cold stiffened fingers pulling at the end of the chute, feeding it from the pack. The slowness—it seemed to him to be in slow motion —was maddening, but each time he tried hurrying the feeding of the chute, his fingers would fumble and he became momentarily paralyzed by the fear that the chute would tangle, fouling on some of his gear, failing to open.

Glancing down again, Frost tugged harder at his chute—feeding it out by the handful until the wind caught it, shooting it up above him, his body going straight. His descent—it wasn't slowing, he realized, glancing upward. The chute—was it his imagination that it wasn't opening? Then suddenly there was a jerk, the pain wrenching through his back and neck as he looked up, the billowing umbrella of nylon above him, his hands automatically going to the guide lines to control his descent. In his heart and mind two things obsessed him. If Karkov dove from the plane, Frost would kill him—if not he'd follow the man to the ends of the earth to get him. He had to be working with the Nazis.

As Frost tumbled into the snow, rolling against the impact and getting to his feet in a low crouch, he hacked with the Gerber at the chute webbing, undoing the buckles when he could, then gathering the chute into his arms. There was a bracken of pines off to his left and he made for them—the second thought burning at him was that he had to urinate or die. A moment later, Frost was on his knees burying the chute beneath the snow, his eye scanning the horizon for signs of Karkov's chute. The silenced Walther P-38K was in his fist as he turned, hearing footsteps crunching in the snow behind him. "It is me," the voice was Marita's.

"You see what happened," Frost almost hissed.

"Yes—your chute. It would not open."

"Karkov," Frost said deliberately.

"It could not be," the girl said.

"I checked the chute myself, and Karkov was the only person I left alone with it after that—I had to see Fouchard. Remember?"

"But it couldn't be him," the girl said.

"I hope it is," Frost said emotionlessly. "I don't want to feel guilty after I kill the bastard—and that's a promise. Now how are the others?"

"Blouchard," she said. "His chute did not open, but the others from the counter-terrorist squad seem to have made it."

"I bet ya' I know who to blame that chute on."

"You are insane—I have fought with Karkov, side by side. He is a Jew—what would he do helping the Nazis?"

"Everybody's got sleeper agents, kid—plants put into an intelligence service who are model agents, dedicated, loyal—until that one job comes along. Karkov couldn't have contacted the castle, to let the Nazis know we were coming. He had to count on sabotaging the chutes, then doing what he could on the ground to stop us. Maybe they got somethin' on him—I don't know. The reason isn't important. And I'll lay odds he's not really a Jew—think about it. He set me up with that bitch at the clock shop— he had to know she'd test J. W. Carlson's sexual preferences, and if Karkov had all that information on Carlson, you'd think a little detail like his being a homosexual would have been included. Karkov was the control—right?"

"But he always is."

"You haven't gone against the Nazi movement before as a team, have you?"

The girl fell silent, Frost turning his eye skyward

205

again, searching the dawn for a sign of Karkov's chute. Then behind him, he heard the girl say, "You must be right – but drop the gun – now!"

Frost started to turn, then her voice came again, "I mean it – you know I'll kill you."

Frost didn't drop the gun – he just looked at her. "What you got in mind?"

"He is one of us – or was. And I will kill him. He will not suspect me." The menace in her voice was something Frost hadn't heard before.

Frost whispered to her, "I'm not dropping the gun – go ahead and kill him, but if you fail I'll be right there backing you up. No other way." He watched the girl nod. Even in the half-light across the snowfield the hardness of her green eyes was unmistakable.

"Let's go," Frost murmured, heading out onto the snowfield, the girl close at his side, the silenced Walther .22 she carried clenched in her gloved right fist. Frost retrieved his drop case and unlimbered the CAR-15, holstering his P-38K.

They trekked a half mile or more before they linked up with the others, then went on, further ahead along the route where – if Karkov had jumped – he would have to be. And surprisingly, for all the guile he had used in tampering with Frost's chute and that of the hapless French policeman, Blouchard, he was waiting in open sight.

"Frost," the man said, starting to come forward. "I saw the problem you were having with your chute – thank God you're alive."

The girl said it, but Frost felt she had read his mind, "Don't add blasphemy to your crimes."

206

"What do you say," Karkov said, edging away. "Where is Blouchard?"

"Where I'm supposed to be," Frost said drily. "He's dead. And he didn't volunteer for that. You fuckin' Nazi," Frost rasped.

"Nazi," Karkov said, his tone of voice incredulous.

"There is no escape, Karkov," the girl said, moving forward from beside Frost.

Frost could see no weapon in her hands. She walked, slowly, slipping slightly once in the snow. Karkov edged away from her, his right hand going to the holster on his belt.

"Look out," Frost shouted to Marita, his own hands starting to swing up the muzzle on the CAR-15.

But Marita's hands were faster. Her right arm flashed forward, nothing in her hand, and then suddenly the black chrome-plated Sting knife was at the tips of her fingers and sailing forward in a straight line, Karkov doubling over and falling to his knees in the snow, his hands clenched to his throat. Frost dropped the muzzle of his rifle and walked up beside the girl, putting his left arm around her shoulders. "I had you figured as being good with a knife," he said mechanically.

Chapter Eighteen

The trek across the snows was difficult, none of the people in Frost's party—he had assumed unofficial command after the death of Karkov—acclimatized to the cold. Contaigne, one of the French policemen, had fallen once, and they'd all rested, Marita warming the man's half frozen feet against the flesh of her abdomen. Frost thought well of the men in the company. No one had said anything. That Marita was a woman—and a beautiful one—was secondary. That she had automaton-like killed the traitor among them at dawn that morning was something no one had even referred to.

Frost watched the girl, her eyes far away as she massaged the French policeman's half frozen feet. "You're quite a girl," was all he said, then he got up and went a few yards up the trail, relieving the man on guard there—one of the Mossad agents. It was colder there, more in the wind. As Frost stood there by the pines, hoping that he blended in with the snow background enough not to represent a target, he munched on a Hershey bar. The CAR-15 was slung from his right shoulder, his right hand holding the pistol grip, the scope covers still in place. He finished the chocolate bar and pulled back his storm sleeve, checking the time. He judged them to be a little more than an hour from the castle. Then he heard the sounds up ahead—footsteps crunching through the snow.

Frost made a low whistle to the people behind him, knowing full well that anyone coming along the trail would have heard it as well.

One of the Mossad men came running up to him with Marita at his side—she was still closing her jacket. "What is it," the girl said, her voice hushed.

"I don't know," Frost said. "Probably German troops or police—someone might have seen the airdrop."

"I'll talk," the young Mossad man said.

In less than two minutes, they could see the first of the column coming toward them—six West German security troopers, a sergeant of some sort in their lead. The Mossad man stepped out of the trees— Frost had his gun ready from a concealed spot in the woods, Marita crouched beside him.

The Mossad man, Berenstein, was speaking in what—at least to Frost—sounded to be perfect German. Frost understood enough of the language to follow the conversation. They were a top secret security force—terrorist activity was reported in the area and they were investigating. The troopers were to move on. Frost didn't necessarily think the real Germans would buy that and he had no desire to open fire on friendly troops. As he followed the conversation, he could tell the Germans weren't buying Berenstein's line.

Frost made a decision, then stood up, walking slowly forward, his CAR-15 raised in the air. Berenstein's face dropped, the Germans raised their weapons. His German not as good as he would have liked, Frost began, "Ich, ah . . . " Fumbling his way along for a moment, one of the Germans—mercifully Frost thought—said, "I speak English. You are American or British?"

Smiling and lowering his CAR-15 slowly, Frost said, "I'm gonna put it right on the line, guys— we're a special United Nations Intelligence team— assigned to penetrate a Communist intelligence base located up there in the mountains. Two of our team are dead—I'm deputizing you guys to help us. You don't have to worry—we're working directly under your own Field Marshall Richter out of U. N. Headquarters. Now let's cut the palaver and get going." Frost turned on his heel and, winking back to Marita, started down the trail. There was no Field Marshall Richter and he hoped the German's didn't know that. From behind him, he heard one of the Germans shouting, "Who are you?"

Frost turned and shouted back over his shoulder, "You can just call me Captain Frost—that's obviously a code name but I'm not allowed to reveal my real identity. But who's in charge."

210

The sergeant—the one Frost had spoken with—came forward. Frost whispered in a low voice to the man, "I'll pledge you to secrecy—I'm really Admiral Lucius Blankenshit of U. S. O. N. I.—but don't say a word." Frost watched the man a moment, then the soldier took a step back and saluted.

Saying, "I shouldn't do this," Frost returned the salute, adding, "I'll mention your perception and grasp of the situation to your superiors, Sergeant. You may find yourself at U. N. Headquarters sooner than you realize—we could use a few men like you. Let's move out."

Frost started up the trail again, heard the German Sergeant shout something to his men and looking over his shoulder, saw them following into step. Marita came up beside him, whispering, "You are crazy—I like you. I like crazy men."

Glancing down at her, Frost said, "You mean when we made love that night it wasn't all for show."

"Not all of it—I was cold."

"So was I," Frost said, lighting a cigarette, his hands cupped around the flame of the Zippo.

"You deputized them?"

"John Wayne—God rest his soul—used to do that all the time. Why can't I?"

She started to grab his arm, then smiled—both of them, Frost felt, remembering she was masquerading as a man for the moment. If you didn't look at the face, under the bulky clothing she might have passed for a short one at that, Frost thought.

Chapter Nineteen

Frost and the others huddled in the rocks across the narrow gorge from the castle. "Is this on some tour—I'd love to see what it looks like inside," Frost quipped to Marita.

"Ohh—be quiet," she whispered. "Now how do we get in—Admiral?"

"Well, I'll just float a frigate or two up that frozen creek down there and—" then interrupting himself, his voice sobering, Frost said, "Got no choice—rapel up the side along there after we make the climb, then go over the wall. I used to read books about knights in armor when I was a kid and I know just how those old castles are set up—have confidence." Frost signalled to the men a few yards behind him and he and Marita started forward.

The climb to the castle – because of geographic necessity – had to start with a climb down into the narrow gorge, but this was made with little difficulty. Crossing the icy stream bed in haste – there was the chance that a guard on the parapets might be glancing down – was trickier. Marita fell and Frost caught her, falling too in the process. The others belly-crawled along the slick ice surface – it was already starting to crack under their weight.

Once past the stream, Frost and the Mossad men broke out the ropes, one of the Sûreté men – Contaigne, the man with the bad feet – volunteering to make the initial climb. "I am a mountain climber by avocation, Captain Frost – I can do it."

"What about the feet?"

"They will serve – I want to get out of the snow first – that's why I want to lead. The man winked and Frost smiled, the toque long since stuffed in his pocket, the skin of his cheeks hurting when he moved his face.

"All right – fine," Frost said. "But I'm the first one after you – then I go over the wall into the castle first – I'm particularly skilled at that sort of thing."

"*Oui* – it is agreed." Contaigne set himself up with the rope slings around his waist and under his rear end, the carabiner clips set, additional coils of rope set about his shoulders, crosshatched like ammunition bandoliers.

Frost and the others crouched motionless beneath the jagged rock face, feeding the rope as Contaigne started up. The going – at least to Frost on the ground below by the edge of the icy stream – seemed torturously slow. And it was, he decided—it took Contaigne nearly a half hour to reach the summit just below the castle wall.

Then Frost nested himself with the ropes and started up, the actual climb with the ropes in place and secured with pitons along the way taking Frost five minutes, mostly because of the slipperiness of the rocks under his combat-booted feet.

As he gained the summit, Frost looked to Contaigne. "You're a tough man, my friend." The Frenchman, his lips almost blue with the cold, merely nodded, his eyes listless. Frost stared at him a moment. "What's wrong?" The man said nothing. On impulse Frost slapped his hand against the side of the man's foot—there was no reflex withdrawal.

"Your feet," Frost muttered, then, Contaigne protesting, Frost undid the laces on the man's right boot, pulled off both socks and looked at the skin—it was nearly black. "My God, man—that could go gangrenous."

"I know—don't tell the others," Contaigne muttered.

"You've been frostbitten before—haven't you?" Frost asked.

"*Oui*—during Korea. But I had to come."

"Do you know what you just did—you could be crippled for life, lose your feet."

"It does not matter," Contaigne said. "My father—he was killed during the War. He hated the Nazis. My mother was Jewish. I am tired what the world press is saying—that not enough of the French care. I care, I am French—I will kill the Nazis!"

Frost replaced the socks and the boot on Contaigne's right foot, saying, "Like I said a minute ago, pal — you're a tough man, my friend."

Frost worked the ropes, then helped Marita and the others up onto the summit at the base of the castle walls. The walls rose thirty feet overhead, and Frost wasn't certain if he dared the use of pitons — the noise the hammer would make. He decided on a gamble and took the launcher one of the Mossad men had strapped to his pack.

Frost freed the rope and the three pronged device for attachment to the rock surface. Rather than mechanically launching it and risk the noise that would entail, he decided to hurl it. "Just like the knights, huh," he said, winking at Marita as he stepped to the edge of the rise and began twirling the long rope overhead.

It made a hissing sound, growing louder as the speed increased. Frost swung, the rope sailing upward, the pronged device missing the top and dropping back down to the ground, barely missing one of the Germans.

"I'll get it this time," Frost said, grinning sheepishly. He started twirling the rope overhead again, this time the rushing sound it made through the air stronger. Then he made the swing, the rope snaking upwards and catching between the parapets.

"Be seein' ya'," Frost rasped, the Gerber boot knife in his teeth as he ran toward the castle wall, jumping up and grabbing at the rope and starting to rapel up the wall.

Hand over hand, Frost climbed the rough rock surface, stopping just below the rim of the wall and peering over the top. There was a lone guard on the wall, and Frost saw men on each of the other three walls as well. Swinging from the rope, he nodded broadly toward Marita's anxious face below — she'd removed the toque, clear now to the Germans that she was a woman, her dark hair cascading to her shoulders.

Swinging round, Frost touched the top of the wall with his left hand, rolling over the edge and onto the walkway. The guard was forty yards away — about to turn back from the end of his tour, Frost saw. He would see the rope, he would see Frost as he crouched by the side of the wall. Snatching the Walther with the silencer from the belt holster at his waist, Frost levelled the weapon and waited.

As the guard turned, Frost fired once — the silencer making the shot little more than a loud, hacking cough, killing the crack as the round broke the sound barrier at least as best as Frost could tell behind the muzzle. The guard's rifle clattered to the stone walkway, his hands clasping his chest, falling forward. Leaning over the side of the wall, he signalled below him, Marita the first to grasp at the rope and start up. Frost didn't wait for her, racing forward along the top of the wall in a low crouch toward the dead guard. Stripping the man of his assault rifle and pistol, pocketing the latter and slinging the rifle across his back, Frost glanced over his shoulder. Marita, hair blowing in the stiff wind, was already over the wall and rushing toward him. So far, Frost saw, the attention of the other guards hadn't been attracted.

Frost scanned the castle grounds below them. There were dozens of vehicles parked near the far wall beside the gates which led to the single access road on the far side of the mountain. In the center of the courtyard was a helipad, marked with lights for night landings, Frost observed. There were three helicopters, two large, military style, like Huey Cobras, the third something similar to a Bell—bubble fronted and designed for no more than four occupants.

Lying flush with the walkway, Frost rasped to Marita beside him, "I'd wager that building is crawling with men—check out all those vehicles. Thank God it's cold or they'd all be out in the courtyard and we'd have been spotted."

"What do we do now?" the girl whispered.

"We gotta split up—one team to set this place for destruction when we leave, one team to glomb onto those helicopters for us to escape—if we can find some pilots."

"I fly," she said. "That West German sergeant —I noticed an airborne qualification badge—he might."

"Whatever," Frost said. "Hell—I wish we would have realized they were that well set up. Anyway —the last team goes after Balsam."

"Contaigne can—"

"He can't do anything—his feet might already be gangrenous," Frost whispered. "Just put him in a good spot with a gun and let him kill people —have somebody to help him walk it out to the helicopters just in case we get out of here alive."

"What now, then?"

Frost looked at the girl. "I'd like to do this with a little greater subtlety, but I don't think we've

217

got the time. Wait a minute," he rasped. His eye caught a technician wearing a white hospital coat running from the north wing of the castle out to the heliport area. Overhead, he could hear rotor blades whirring. He looked up – a small helicopter like the one already on the ground between the two military ships. As the machine hovered over the grounds – Frost and Marita keeping their heads down, their bodies pressed against the walkway – Frost glanced back to the technician. The man was waiting at the edge of the landing area, his arms slapping against his sides against the cold.

As the chopper landed, the man ran toward it, Frost propping himself up now on one elbow. The cold – from lying still for so long – was starting to penetrate his clothing. He was shivering. The technician took a small suitcase from the pilot of the helicopter and – ducking needlessly under the rotor blades – ran back in through the door he'd come from. "Hospital wing," Frost rasped. "They'll have Balsam in there. I'm gonna bet on it."

Frost and Marita edged back along the wall, where Berenstein, Contaigne – his face gray and sick looking – the West German soldiers, and the other waited. The West German sergeant said, "My God – is this a military base?"

"I may as well tell you the truth," Frost said. "This is a base – but for the neo-Nazis. They're holding an old Jewish professor down there, torturing him to reveal the names of people in the European anti-Nazi movement. They're not Communists. You've come this far – you gonna help us?"

218

The sergeant looked at Frost a moment, then at his five men. "We will," he whispered, nodding.

"Good," Frost said. "Here's what we do."

The plan was simple—much as Frost had outlined it to the girl before the arrival of the fourth helicopter. Only now there was direction to it, Frost thought as he detailed it. Happily, he learned, the West German could fly a helicopter. Marita was surprised to learn that Berenstein could as well —he didn't have a license yet, but was nearly through with his lessons. Frost made a mental note not to ask whether he'd covered landings yet.

Berenstein would go with the West Germans to secure the helipad and at least three of the choppers. Contaigne was put in charge of the fire element on the wall they now occupied. Frost and Marita were the second maneuver element. With several of the Mossad people they would penetrate the hospital wing—or at least what Frost hoped was the hospital wing; then attempt the rescue of Balsam. On the way out, they'd split and sabotage the place.

Marita beside and slightly behind him, Frost started down along the walkway, at any moment knowing that their phenomenal luck of no one having noticed the missing guard there would end.

And it did.

Chapter Twenty

Frost was halfway down the crude stone steps leading to the castle courtyard and toward the helipad, looming beyond it was the entrance to the assumed hospital wing. Frost turned when he heard the shout. The words were in German and he didn't catch them well enough to understand, but the meaning was clear. There wasn't time to telescope out the stock on the CAR-15 in his hands; he just swung the muzzle up and snapped off two quick shots toward the guard on the far wall who'd shouted the alarm, the man crumpling, his body jerking twice as the 5.56mm slugs hammered into his center of mass. Frost swung the muzzle of the Colt toward the helipad and broke into a run down the steps, jumping the last three, going into a crouch and firing at the nearest guards.

Gunfire was everywhere now, Contaigne's men on the wall spraying the courtyard with automatic weapons fire as Nazis streamed – it seemed without end – from the castle building itself. "Come on!" Frost shouted to Marita and the others with him.

Getting to his feet and breaking into a dead run toward the door to the hospital wing, Frost kept up a steady barage of gunfire – the rank of Nazis building up just beyond the helipad was seemingly impenetrable. From the corner of his eye, he could see Marita running in a low crouch, the muzzle of her Uzi streaming fire.

One of the Mossad agents went down, and over the din of gunfire, Frost heard the man shout to Marita, "Kill me!" Frost glanced at him – his abdomen and chest were a mass of gunshot wounds and death. As Marita turned and levelled her pistol toward the dying man's head, Frost pushed her away, pulling the pistol from his belt and shooting the man once in the head.

Her eyes caught his eye a moment, then they ran on. As they reached the hospital wing door, Frost pushed Marita through behind three of the Mossad agents, punching out the stock on his rifle and – sighting through the scope – emptying his magazine at targets of opportunity on the far walls. When the CAR-15 came up empty, Frost nearly dove through the doorway, a hail of submachine gun fire from the Nazis pulverizing the wall around him.

Inside, Frost pressed himself against the interior wall, changing magazines on the CAR-15, chambering a round and shortening the stock again.

"You ready?" Marita said quietly.

"Uh-huh," Frost said, nodding, biting his lower lip a moment. "Yeah—let's go!"

Frost started off down the passageway, the stone castle walls lit with bare bulb fixtures via exposed wiring. An alarm started sounding, like an air raid siren, audible through speakers placed at long intervals throughout the length of the passageway. Once, in anger, Frost smashed the buttstock of his CAR-15 into one of the speakers, knocking it in pieces from the wall.

As Frost, Marita and the others rounded a bend in the tunnel, he spotted a hazy cloud rolling toward them— "Gas!" he screamed, reaching to his pack and snatching a mask from the webbing pouch affixed there. Frost ripped the black stocking cap from his head—the rolled up toque—and pressed the mask over his face, securing the straps, then popping the sides of the mask at the cheeks as he breathed out, sealing the mask.

Glancing over his shoulder, he could see Marita and the others doing the same. There was no choice but to race through the gas cloud, hoping it was something that would not grossly effect the skin and poison through contact—like a nerve gas.

Seeing was almost impossible, and once into the cloud they felt their way along the tunnel passageway with their hands pressed against the rock surface. At the edge of the gas cloud, Frost skidded to a halt, three hazy-looking figures at the fringe of the cloud, looming ahead of them. In an instant, the three figures had opened fire. Dropping into

222

a crouch, Frost began firing the CAR-15, Marita beside him, her Uzi firing short, rapid bursts. The noise of gunfire in the confined passageway was deafening, hot brass ricocheting off the walls and pelting the hands and the surfaces of the gas masks Frost, Marita and the others wore. Ricochets of the fired rounds bounced and whined off the walls, one of the Mossad men catching a burst of rock chips in his left arm.

Frost looked behind him, waving his left hand for the firing to cease—the three subgunners at the fringe of the gas cloud were down—dead, Frost assumed. He started running again. They went on, Frost gauged, for another two or three minutes, the passage taking them down under the castle, no further resistance in evidence. The sirens were still wailing through the wall-mounted speakers. Slowing then to a quick commando walk, they rounded another bend in the passageway, Frost stopping abruptly, retreating around the passage wall. Using hand signals, he told the others he had seen four men—armed—by large double swinging doors. It was hot breathing inside the gas mask, but reason told him that there might be more gas waiting for them ahead and to keep the masks in place.

Frost signalled—again using his hands—that they would attack the four men at the count of three. Using his left hand, he broadly raised one finger, then a second, then a third. Frost, Marita and the others stepped around the bend in the passage. Frost fell into a crouch, all of them opening up with their automatic and semi-automatic weapons at the four submachine gun armed Nazis at the

223

end of the passage by the double doors.

Two of the Nazis went down immediately, the third — shot-through — spreadeagling and falling back through the swinging doors, which splintered under Marita's fire with the 9mm Uzi. The fourth man was still shooting, on his knees, the subgun in his hands firing as though the trigger were held in a death grip. Frost hip shot the CAR-15 he held, placing a single slug in the man's forehead, driving him back against the wall . . . dead.

Waving his left hand for the others to follow, Frost charged down the passageway toward ·the double doors. They swung open as he was within a yard of them, a black-clad Nazi subgunner opening up from just inside the room. Frost dove to the passage floor and rolled, his CAR-15 coming up on line, firing it one-handed like a pistol, two quick shots catching the subgunner in the midsection and doubling him over, the weapon in his hands still firing as he died.

Frost was on his feet again, Marita passing him up and running headlong through the doors.

It was the hospital wing — small operating enclosures, a few beds along a short hallway. Frost came abreast of Marita as they reached the far wall, then both turned, another set of double doors before them. As if of one mind, Frost thought, they both slowed, approached the swinging double doors from the sides. When Marita nodded, each kicked in a door, Frost rolling into the room and coming up on his knees, the CAR-15 ready, Marita dropping into a crouch, the Uzi at the ready, just inside the right hand door.

It was as though, Frost thought, someone had shouted, "Freeze!" like children do in a school-yard game. Balsam—though hardly recognizable for the bruises and abrasions on his face—lay on the operating table. A white coated man—wearing one of those silver discs with an eyehole on a sweatband on his forehead—stood over Balsam, a blood-dripping scalpel in his rubber gloved right hand, the glove smeared red. A woman sat on a small stool beside the near end of the operating table, a steno pad on her knee, a pencil in her hand. A tape recorder was running by the head of the operating table. Balsam, his speech garbled—drugged, Frost wondered—was mumbling something in German. And Liebling and one other Nazi, standing beside the near end of the table, were turned, facing Frost and Marita.

No one moved for an instant, then Liebling—in English—started to say, "Please do not shoot." Ripping the gas mask from his face so Liebling could remember him, Frost squeezed the trigger on the assault rifle in his right fist and shot Liebling twice in the mouth, the Nazi's body toppling to the floor like a rotted tree struck by lightning.

Frost glanced toward Marita—the silenced Walther .22 was in her right hand, the Uzi in her left now, the Walther raised in a classic target-like position. Frost's eye rivetted to her as she fired—once, the Nazi who had stood next to Liebling pulling his hands up to his neck as he fell forward—then twice, the doctor, his bloody hand streaking toward his right eye as he collapsed across the operating table and over Balsam's body. As Marita levelled the pistol toward the stenographer, Frost shouted, "No—don't be like them!"

Marita looked at Frost, lowered the pistol and rasped something in German that he didn't make out. The stenographer dropped the pad and pencil to the floor and ran from the room.

"She could have Professor Balsam's information, Frost."

"Balsam didn't say anything," Frost whispered, walking toward the table and shoving the body of the dead medic off Balsam and onto the floor. The old professor was an almost unrecognizable pulp. What the Nazis hadn't known, Frost realized, was that Balsam was under a close death sentence already—nothing they could have done, Frost realized, short of a truth drug (and Frost wondered if that would have even worked) could have caused Balsam to reveal what he knew of the anti-Nazi movement in Europe.

Marita came around the far side of the table, searched the medical cabinets mounted to the walls and turned toward Balsam, a hypodermic and a bottle of some type of liquid in her hands. She filled the hypo expertly, then bent over Balsam. "Wait," Frost rasped.

"I'm not going to kill him—I'm trying to ease his pain—he's virtually dead already. I'm not a butcher."

Frost didn't interfere as the Mossad agent touched the needle to the inside of Balsam's left forearm. She raised the blanket like operating tent and peered under it, then turned her head away. Frost looked away, hearing the sound of the girl throwing up on the floor.

He turned back, hearing Balsam trying to speak. "I—told . . ."

"I know," Frost said, his voice soft. "You told them nothing."

"Yes," Balsam coughed. "Nothing—nothing. Arsenal—beyond wall, I—think." Balsam closed his eyes.

"Is he dead?" Frost said, glancing up at Marita. Her face was white. She touched her fingers to Balsam's neck, then nodded, "No."

"Wait here," Frost said, glancing over his shoulder, seeing the rest of the Mossad agents by the door. "You," Frost shouted to one of the men, gesturing for him to follow.

Frost ran out of the room, toward the far door where the stenographer had gone. It was a continuation of the same passage, apparently, but the angle went decidedly upward. There was a small metal door a few yards along the passage and Frost ran toward it. But it was chained shut with a modern combination padlock.

"Here, give me that," Frost said, turning to the Mossad man beside him, handing the man his CAR-15 and taking the Uzi.

Frost gestured for the man to stand back, then getting off to an angle himself to avoid ricochet, Frost fired a long burst from the Uzi into the padlock. The lock held. Frost fired another burst, the lock finally snapping and falling to the floor.

Frost moved to the door and stripped the chain away, then pushed it open—it swung in. The room was packed, floor to ceiling, with small arms ammunition, boxes of explosives, grenades and mor-

227

tar rounds. Lining the walls were racks of modern assault rifles, submachine guns, even a small rack of pistols.

"See anything you like?" Frost said.

The Mossad man, his gas mask removed like Frost, just shook his head, smiling.

"Me too," Frost said, "although a couple of pocketsful of grenades might be nice to bring to the folks back home though, huh?"

Frost and the Mossad man each took as many grenades as they could carry. Then Frost found a U. S. surplus Bazooka. "Hey, this would be good," the Mossad man enthused.

"Yeah," Frost groaned, "pity, but I'm gonna need it here—simplest way to make all this stuff go up."

Frost pried at the rocket launcher with his knife and got to the electrical wiring in the control box, verifying that the contacts worked and carried a charge. Taking a bale of barbed wire, he connected the end to the right lead, put a rocket down the tube, ready to fire. Then he stuffed the forward portion of the tube with grenades, the pins pulled. "Come on," Frost rasped to the Mossad man as he ran the barbed wire back down the hall and into the medical wing, stopping alongside Marita and Balsam.

"Doc," Frost rasped, as he pulled a light from a wall outlet, then using the small Gerber stripped the plug from it.

Balsam groaned.

"Could you," Frost said," blow this whole place for us—just putting two wires together?"

The old man's eyes opened, a light shining in them that Frost felt very good about just then.

"What are you doing?" Marita asked.

"Bazookas—at least the U. S. kind—fire by electrical impulse, right? Well, this one's gonna go big." Taking medical adhesive, Frost wrapped the ends of the wires, telling Marita, "Put rubber gloves on the Doc's hands, just for added protection."

Frost finished the wiring as Marita gloved the injured old man. Turning to Balsam, Frost said, "Doctor Balsam—you know you're dying, Sir," and the man nodded. "You can strike a final blow against the Nazis: when we leave, count to fifty. Just touch these two exposed wires together and hold them—the blast should kill you, too. You want to do it?"

Balsam mumbled, "Yes."

"If you start feeling like your passing out—don't wait until you reach fifty—just do it. This is the hot one," Frost showed the man the wire leading from the wall outlet. The rubber glove over the stump of Balsam's left hand looked bizarrely absurd, and Marita had to tape the wire lead to Balsam's thumb so he could control it.

"You ready," Frost asked Marita. She nodded, touched her hand to Balsam's cheek and started toward the doors, gesturing to the Mossad men to come with her.

Frost turned to Balsam. "Doctor—I'm sorry it went like this. But if you wanted to make the world a good bit more conscious of the Nazi threat—if its any comfort, I think you succeeded."

The old man, his lips parched and cracked, forced

a smile. Frost bent his head to listen as he whispered, "God bless you." The man's breath smelled like death, Frost thought, but somehow it didn't bother him.

Smiling, Frost touched the old professor's hand and whispered, "And God bless you too, Sir." Then Frost started to run, behind him hearing the murmuring of the old man starting to count. Frost counted, too.

He reached Marita and the others at the count of three, waved for them to hurry beside him. Racing up the corridor, he mentally ticked off the number eight as he passed the armory room. There was a bend in the corridor ahead, which they reached at the count of fourteen. At the count of twenty-three, Frost and the others stopped, a phalanx of submachine gun armed Nazis coming down the corridor toward them. Frost and the others with him opened fire, one of the Mossad men, the man who had been wounded by the rock chips, catching a burst square in the chest and going down dead.

As they started running again, Frost reckoned the count at forty-one.

Forty-two – they rounded another bend, the passage steeper now and taking them up into the castle. Forty-three – they passed a small room, the doorway opened and two Nazis inside. Frost fired point blank, stopping and sidetracking into the room. Forty-four and forty-five – "The treasury – I got the diamonds," Frost shouted, running from the room, the original package, one end taped closed after being ripped open, under his arm.

Forty-six — they were running again. Forty-seven, forty-eight, forty-nine — Frost, in the lead beside Marita, spotted the end of the passage, leading into a large vaulted hall, beyond it, visible now, an open walkway leading toward the courtyard.

"Fifty!" Frost shouted, running as fast as he could along the end of the passage. Behind them, a moment later, Frost heard the roar of the explosion building in force — it seemed — right at their heels.

Chapter Twenty-one

Halfway along the length of the high vaulted castle hall, Frost glanced over his shoulder, shouting, "Pour it on – pour it on !"

Behind him, he could see the fireball roaring up the passageway, the castle floor trembling beneath his feet, the walls on the near side starting to shake and crumble. Debris was already starting to fall as Frost and the others reached the end of the long hall and hit the courtyard.

Gunfire, mortar bursts, hand grenade explosions were everywhere. Frost turned, then threw himself to the ground, pulling Marita down beside him, some of the others running past – blown forward as the impact of the arsenal explosion belched out of the castle and tore the walls of the building down behind

232

them. The roar was deafening, Frost pressing his hands to his ears, his body half on top of Marita.

Shaking his head to clear it, burning debris falling from his back as he stood, Frost was stunned by the silence. He snapped his fingers—he could still hear, but for the moment all gunfire had stopped. Suddenly then, he looked behind him. Grabbing Marita up from the ground and pulling her forward further into the courtyard, he saw the nearest of the main castle walls tumbling outward, the high spires on the roof collapsing into the structure, smoke belching up from the ground as the centuries-old rock slabs collapsed.

Frost stopped running—they were beside the closest of the helicopters, one of the smaller bubble-domed machines. Frost shouted to the girl, his ears still ringing, "I don't know what the hell kind of explosives they had in there, but I never expected all that!"

"Poor Balsam," she half screamed, and Frost nodded. The gunfire was starting up again and Frost pushed Marita toward the helicopter, bending down and snatching up submachine guns from the fallen men along the ground near the helipad.

"Get aboard!" he shouted.

Already, from the corner of his eye, Frost could see the West German sergeant and some of the others starting toward one of the larger military helicopters.

As Frost climbed aboard the smaller chopper, Marita was already warming the rotors. With the blades turning lazily overhead, Frost turned and fired, a squad of Nazis running toward them, their subguns blazing. "Get this damned thing off the ground!" Frost shouted.

"I can't," The girl screamed back. "I need another minute or so to build up RPMs."

Frost climbed back out of the chopper, dropping to one knee and firing the subgun in his hands until it was empty. He snatched another gun off the ground and kept firing. It too ran dry. He looked over his shoulder, Marita waving frantically to him. As he started aboard, he peeled the CAR-15 from his back and kept firing. The chopper starting to climb now, Frost hurtled his load of hand grenades down into the Nazis below him, strafing the ground with the CAR-15 through the swirling mass of snow and debris kicked up by the wind of the rotors.

Turning and looking forward, Frost saw the far castle wall looming in front of them out of the corner of his eye, seeing Marita frantically working the controls of the helicopter, the machine gliding upward mere feet from the wall, then sinking down again, then starting to climb to get past the far bank of the gorge, the frozen stream below them now.

Frost started to tell the girl to turn back so he could provide covering fire for the others, but behind him he could see one of the large gunships coming up over the wall, a recognizable face leaning out the side door, one of the Mossad men firing a submachine gun back into the castle grounds.

The larger helicopter easily overtook them, and as it did Frost could see the West German sergeant giving an "okay" sign. Marita waved back as the ship passed them by.

"Home free!" Frost said, then turned and looked behind them. Already, the ship commanded by the West German was nearly out of sight, but looming up from the rubble of the castle, Frost saw one more gunship. "Nazis!" he rasped.

Chapter Twenty-Two

As the helicopter gunship closed from behind, the coaxially mounted machine guns along its fuselage opened fire, Frost returning fire with the remaining subguns he had aboard, knowing full well that it was a futile gesture. No weapon he had was a match for the range or cyclic rate of the guns mounted on the Nazi chopper.

Glancing ahead of them—Marita working the controls for evasive action—Frost could see the other gunship, the West German at its controls, speeding back toward them, its guns already blazing.

Marita, beside Frost, shouted, "We're hit!" Already, he could smell the acrid smoke of burning oil, the whirring of the blades overhead becoming

236

erratic, the wind around the small helicopter humming as they cut downward through the air.

"Brace yourself!" she screamed, the runners of the chopper clipping against the snowladen tops of the pine trees. Frost watched, almost paralyzed because he could do nothing as she worked at the controls. Looking below then, the snow was coming up fast—they impacted.

Shaking her head, Frost watched as the girl shouted, "Get out—before she blows!"

Frost rolled out of the open cockpit and into the snow, crawling on his hands and knees as he pulled himself to his feet, running then and falling, the pressure behind his back like the hand of a giant knocking him to the ground, the roar of the explosion hammering at his ears, his hands going up to protect his head.

He rolled over. Beyond the blazing wreckage of the chopper, the burning trees beside it, he could see Marita, standing already, holding her left shoulder, her face—even at the distance—smudged and dirty.

Frost got to his feet and walked across the snow toward her. As he reached her, he pulled her into his arms, going into a crouch. The air vibrated with another explosion. And as the sound died away, he looked up. It was the Nazi gunship—or had been. Far off toward the horizon, Frost could see the ship piloted by the West German, banking and coming back toward them. With his free left arm, Frost started waving to it.

Looking down at the girl in his arms—her body half trembling with cold and shock, Frost whispered

"You know—I seriously think you should give up this spy stuff and become a helicopter pilot. You're really quite good."

As he started walking her toward the center of the clearing, the helicopter with the West German at the controls already homing toward them, the Frenchman Contaigne waving from the open door, Frost began to talk to her. "We can give the diamonds I got in my pack to the people Balsam worked with— the anti-Nazis. He would have wanted that. Can you take some time off—it might take at least a week to find them?"

The girl looked up at him, a smile on her drawn thin lips, "You want to make love with me again?"

"That was the general idea," Frost said.

He smiled as he pulled the girl closer to him, but then the smile faded. Clearly, in his mind's eye, he could see Professor Balsam, remembering the smiling eyes, and then how suddenly they had gone serious— that time they had spoken aboard the flight to Paris. He'd been talking of the Nazis, and loosely quoted the philosopher Santayana, saying, "Those who do not learn the lessons of history shall be forced to relive them."

Frost wondered, the snow from the rotor blades blowing up into his face as he walked the girl toward the helicopter, if Balsam had somehow just given the world a history lesson . . .

GREAT BOOKS

E-BOOKS

AUDIOBOOKS

& MORE

Visit us today

www.speakingvolumes.us